In
Search
of the
Messiah

WHAT THE BIBLE

In

TEACHES

Search

ABOUT GOD,

of the

HIS SON,

Messiah

AND HIS PEOPLE.

Jay Simons

REVIEW AND HERALD® PUBLISHING ASSOCIATION
HAGERSTOWN, MD 21740

The author assumes full responsibility for the accuracy of all facts
and quotations as cited in this book.

This book was
Edited by Gerald Wheeler
Designed by Patricia S. Wegh
Cover design by Bryan Gray
Typeset: 11.5/14 Cochin

PRINTED IN U.S.A.

98 97 96 95 94   10 9 8 7 6 5 4 3 2 1

R&H Cataloging Service
Simons, Jay
    In search of the Messiah.

    1. Jesus Christ—Prophecies. 2. God.
3. Judaism—Relations—Christianity. 4.
Christianity and other religions—Judaism.
I. Title.
            261.26

ISBN 0-8280-0814-0

Contents

Chapter 1 Jay's Quest /7

Chapter 2 Guideposts /18

Chapter 3 Which Bible to Use? /23

Chapter 4 What Is God's Name? /31

Chapter 5 The Son's Name /54

Chapter 6 The Unity of God /79

Chapter 7 The Messiah in Prophecy /91

Chapter 8 Jesus the Messiah /105

Chapter 9 The Lamb of God /115

Chapter 10 The Jewishness of Jesus /122

Chapter 11 People of the Covenant /135

1

Jay's Quest

All my life I have been a questioner. As a young child I continually asked "Why?" and if the answer I received did not seem logical to my limited understanding, I kept questioning until I felt I understood completely. My parents naturally viewed this trait with a great deal of consternation, for many times they did not know the answer either.

Because we were children of a religiously mixed marriage—my father had been raised an Orthodox Jew by Russian and Lithuanian immigrant parents, and my mother had been baptized a Christian as an infant in the Presbyterian Church—my parents exposed my two sisters and me to both religions and gave us the opportunity to make our own decisions. Although our home taught no formal doctrine of either faith, we celebrated all the holidays—Christian and Jewish. My parents also instructed us in the Ten Commandments and provided a good moral structure. Our formal religious education came from both churches and synagogues. Since our parents stayed neutral, and neither of them professed a strong religious belief to us, they sent us initially to the First Church Congregational in Bradford, Massachusetts, until we entered high school, and then to Temple Emanuel in Haverhill, Massachusetts, to complete our religious education.

Though they hoped to provide a broad base for us on which to choose our future course, it actually confused me by opening more doors and posing more questions for which I began a lifelong search for answers. I thoroughly enjoyed attending all the religious ceremonies—especially those of the Catholic Church—with my schoolmates. The rituals, pomp, and mystery associated with the cathedrals, priesthood, and nuns fascinated me.

My search for identity and answers to life's mysteries took me to the far corners of various religious communities and philosophies.

My paternal grandparents, Max and Fannie Cortell, were Orthodox Jews. When my parents married, Bubbie and Zadie (as we later called them) turned the mirrors to the walls and sat *shivah* (mourning for the dead) for my father. They kept a kosher house, never eating meat and dairy dishes at the same meal, and only those foods that conformed to Mosaic health laws.

After seeing that my mother was a good and honest woman—though a Gentile—they began to visit my parents, especially after we girls were born, though they refused to eat in our house. To a little girl, my grandparents were dark and mysterious people—foreboding compared with the lighthearted Irish relatives on Mother's side. I enjoyed both sets of relatives for who they were—and they were all good and honest people.

On Saturday nights, after my father had locked up his Army/Navy store, we would all go to the delicatessen my grandfather's brother Mike ran in the old Jewish section of Haverhill, near the Orthodox *shul* (synagogue). Everything there was kosher—the corned beef, salami, and the dill pickles in the big wooden barrel. The old worn wooden counters with the ball of string and white wrapping paper are inscribed indelibly in my mind. To me, being Jewish was more of the palate and stomach than a religious doctrine or philosophy at that point in my life. Rituals added to the mystery of Jewishness. But as I grew older I wanted to get below that surface to the reasons for the rituals. Few knew why we did them. "It's what you do. It's tradition. Don't ask why. Just do it. You don't need to know," they would tell me.

So when everyone else in my family—my parents, my grandparents, my sisters, and later my and their husbands—took religion and religious practices at face value, why did I find myself driven to know the reason for everything?

I learned the Bible stories at Sunday school and felt the love of Jesus toward little children. When I entered the seventh grade, I still attended church and my knowledge of the stories (not the Bible) prompted the adult teachers to encourage me to instruct the younger children. But when my father said it was time for me to go to temple and learn about the Old Testament and the Jewish religion, I was fascinated. To me, it was a sign of "growing up," a rite of passage.

But when I began Sabbath school, no one ever mentioned the name of Jesus. During one of my Hebrew classes I asked the instructor why. He replied that Jesus was in the New Testament and that for Jews the Hebrew Scripture (the Old Testament) was the only Bible. When I questioned why so many people believed that Jesus was the Son of God, he said, "For the Jew, Jesus does not exist. In fact, Jesus is the reason the Jews have been persecuted throughout history." He explained that Christians blame the Jews for killing Jesus and that they believe that Jews sacrifice Christian children and drink their blood during the Jewish holidays and in Jewish ritual ceremonies.

This horrified me. I had heard Christians talk about the Jews killing Jesus, but never anything about drinking the blood of Christian children. But then, Jewish children spoke of Christians eating the flesh and drinking the blood of Jesus during Communion, so I became thoroughly confused from both sides. But I continued to ask questions and study at the temple, and became familiar with the customs and doctrines of both Jews and Christians alike.

At the age of 13 when all my classmates were becoming bar or bas mitzvah and accepting their religious duties and place in the family of Jews, I instead stood up on the dais and told the assembly that I was not ready to profess my faith—at least not completely. I still had too many questions that neither my teachers nor the rabbis had been able to answer. Naturally it embarrassed my parents and sisters, who were proudly awaiting my own speech and recitation of the Hebrew prayers and other Jewish writings I had memorized. Not really wanting to hurt anyone, I just stated the facts as I saw them.

Being introduced to Christ first and the prophets second had left me greatly confused. Despite my 12 years of study, I felt my knowledge was superficial, based as it was upon Bible stories for the young. It lacked the maturity and depth I desired. So when I entered Boston University at the age of 16, instead of identifying with one religion or the other, I attended the Hillel House gatherings to maintain my Jewish connections, but also went to Catholic, Protestant, and Baha'i meetings, eagerly listening to each minister, priest, and rabbi to find out the secrets of life and the universe.

Believing firmly in a Higher Power—God—I have always been a seeker of truth. But because so many call Him by different names and view Him in often conflicting ways, I wondered where the truth really lay—or even if there was one truth. After all, each group stated that they were the true believers and that their religion was the repository of all knowledge.

I enrolled in classes in comparative theology, trying to sort through the maze of religious doctrines and philosophies. In my study I traced the history of the development of all religion—from paganism through Judaism, Christianity, Islam, and all its other manifestations. When I finished reading many volumes on the subject, I found myself even more confused than before, and felt that travel would broaden my outlook on life.

Eventually I toured Europe, South America, and the Caribbean islands, searching for truth in synagogues, churches, and cathedrals. I even investigated voodoo. In Haiti, while living with a college roommate whose father was an African ambassador to the country, I began studying a Catholic catechism. But as the date for my baptism approached, a voice inside me told me to return home to my roots.

Starting with my hometown rabbi, Abraham Isaac Jacobson of Temple Emanuel in Haverhill, Massachusetts, I set about learning my heritage as a member of the "chosen people of God." Months turned into years, and I practically lived at the temple in the rabbi's study, searching, studying, arguing. I began to see the purpose of life—who humanity was and why God paid attention to such seemingly insignificant creatures.

In Boston I pursued Rabbi Roland Gittlesohn at Temple Israel, attending Friday night and Sabbath services, dogging him, listening intently to his particular brand of Reform Judaism. My hometown rabbi dished up the Conservative thought. My study so enthralled me that I decided to become a rabbi. Jacobson told me paternalistically, "Be a *rebbitzin* [the wife of a rabbi], or better yet, be a rabbi to your children. The rabbinate is not yet ready to accept woman rabbis," he added. Perhaps his advice was good—even though Judaism later ordained women as rabbis—because it prolonged my quest.

I spent the high holy days at Temple Ohabei Shalom in Newton, Massachusetts, with my father's cousin and his family, thoroughly enjoying the familial feeling and our Jewishness together. When I went to New York City, I sought the rabbis at Temple Israel. There I also went from synagogue to synagogue listening to the sermons, searching for truth.

At 21 I made my decision to become confirmed into the Jewish faith, believing in the writings of the Hebrew Scriptures and in the message the prophets had for our people in those days. But I still wondered about Jesus. My Jewish relatives and friends longed for someone we called the Messiah. Could Jesus be the Messiah, as Christians claimed?

Throughout my college days I always attended Friday night and Sabbath services at Temple Ohabei Shalom in Boston. Though I had originally planned to complete the four-year curriculum in business administration, I was offered a job editing a company publication at a salary I would have received with a B.A. degree. So I took my associate degree from Boston University and entered the publishing field.

Living in an apartment in Harvard Square in Cambridge, I continued my education at Harvard University, taking night classes in European painting, Russian, and German. I also took courses in art at the Museum School and in public relations and communications at Boston University.

During this time someone asked me to be a tour guide for a group of senior citizens touring Europe. We would be visiting cathedrals and churches in Holland, England, Germany, and Italy, where the works of art I had been studying about were on display. Naturally I jumped at the chance.

A boyfriend had given me a silver *mezuzah* on a chain as a going-away gift, and I wore it around my neck. As our group cruised down one of the canals in Amsterdam, another guide pointed out the old Jewish section. He said that most of its inhabitants had perished during World War II, but Dutch citizens had protected many, and they continued to live there today. Motioning to a group of buildings, he added that Jewish people had a market there. I made a mental note of the location, and when our tour group disembarked, I told them to spend the rest of the day shopping, as I wanted to investigate that section.

Unfortunately I soon became lost and began to sense a growing attention from the local boys and men. Wanting to find the Jewish section yet beginning to feel unsafe, I tried to get my bearings to head back to the tour bus. A husky blond young man grabbed my arm and reached for my throat. Instantly I was afraid.

"Juden," he said in German, pointing to my *mezuzah*. "Jew," I translated to myself. He reached into his shirt and pulled out his own *mezuzah*. We felt an immediate connection. Suddenly I felt safe with him. When I explained where I wanted to go, he took me there. Fascinated, I walked between the goods on display, and though I was thousands of miles from home, I felt I was with family.

The young man and I boarded a bus and went to an

Orthodox synagogue outside the city. Going upstairs to the women's section, I looked down on the ark with its Torah scrolls. It seemed just like the old *shul* at home, though larger. I spent the remainder of the afternoon with the fellow, and then he returned me to my group. *Jews,* I thought to myself, *are a family the world over.*

Several years later I married a fellow from New York. I had set out to find a Jewish boy to marry, and he met all the qualifications. Though we had known each other only a short time, he had attended temple services with me, an absolute must because I wanted to marry only a religious person. At that time I did not realize there are those who are pious (who follow the rituals religiously), those who attend religious services out of habit or a sense of loyalty to the traditions of their families, and those who are what I call "stomach Jews"—they eat bagels, lox, knishes, and gefilte fish and consider themselves Jewish. Some of us consider ourselves Jewish for several or all those reasons. Our religious development isn't complete.

We bought a house in Sharon, Massachusetts, and I gave birth to our first child, a daughter we named Tova Rachel (a name symbolizing a good day in my life and a gift from God). My husband and I continued to attend temple. When we moved to Madison, Wisconsin, three years later, we bought a farm in nearby Stoughton. At Temple Beth-El in Madison I taught Sabbath school to the youngsters.

Settling into farm life, I began raising gardens as I had in Sharon, but of a size large enough to feed our family except for only a few items we had to purchase from the store. After we added chickens, ducks, turkeys, sheep, and beef cattle plus a couple milk cows, the farm seemed almost like heaven.

After 12 years, however, our marriage came to an end.

My husband was a television director working in communications at the nearby university, and it seemed we were constantly involved in internal and external power struggles, each trying to discover just what we wanted for our lives and what we needed to survive emotionally and spiritually. I could no longer live a lie of presenting a Jewish identity to the world, keeping kosher at home yet eating *trafe* (nonkosher) food at restaurants. While I wanted a deeper meaning to what I was doing, it seemed that he didn't.

I was not looking for a husband following my divorce, but rather needed to find a way I could raise my two young daughters and stay at home on the farm. We had become foster parents for the state of Wisconsin and Dane County prior to the divorce, and I thoroughly enjoyed taking care of children. For that reason I added a brother and sister whose mother was having problems caring for her children to the infant and 6-year-old I was already keeping.

Happy doing parenting and farming, I thought I had no need for any man in my life. I took the children to their respective religious services on Saturday and Sunday, and also served as room mother at school. I became Brownie and Girl Scout leader, and then got involved in 4-H. It was a full life — until I met a local man of Norwegian-German background who tugged at my heart. Sensitive not only to my inner needs but those of my children, he attracted me both physically and emotionally. We never discussed God as such, and I just assumed, because of his quiet manner and the way he spoke, that he was a religious person. Since then I have learned that each person develops at a different rate and in a different direction.

Marrying, we moved to a homestead in Montana on a mountain where there was no visible evidence of other life than our own immediate family. Trees surrounded us, and the big sky covered our heads. It was here where God, through His Word, spoke to me in a special way.

Our neighbors—Jerry and Yvonne Eller and their family—are Seventh-day Adventists. Only their love for God surpasses their devotion to one another, their children, and their extended family. Family-oriented, they do everything together, always keeping God in the forefront of their lives. The Ellers and their friends Dick and Jane Hartenstein and Jack and Trudy Long live their lives in accordance with God's commandments. And even though I thought I was doing it as well, I began to wonder what they had in their lives that kept them faithful even when awesome tragedies seemed to stalk them.

One day as I explained that I was Jewish, they said, "Oh, we are too." And when I responded "But I thought you were Seventh-day Adventist Christians," they said, "It says in the Bible that if we keep commandments and have the testimony of Jesus, then we are Abraham's seed and heirs to the promise."

That peaked my curiosity and that of my husband, Ben, who, though he had attended Sunday school as a youngster, had not settled onto any religious philosophy of his own. We both expressed an interest in learning more about what these fine people believed in. Jack and Trudy Long offered to study the Bible with us. "The Bible says to search the Scriptures," Jack Long said, "and we will allow it to reveal the truth to you through its writings rather than you asking us what you want to know and us giving you our own thoughts."

That began a series of 30 studies that took us all the way through the Old and New Testaments. Before then I had thought I was well versed in Scripture, but not until we got into it night after night did I learn from the writings of the prophets just what I wanted to know all these years—who God is, what He expects from me and His people, and what the future holds. I had been in search of the Messiah whom Scripture so often speaks about, but I did not know that at the time. Now at last I was finding Him.

The answers I had sought during all those years of studying became crystal clear during our several months of deep seeking. I know now why my quest had taken so long. Out of it came the conclusion that the Lord's special love for the Jewish people—His nation of priests—demands a response. It is our responsibility to teach our people—like that of the prophets before us—of our special duties to love God, to love one another, and to bring the message of God to all generations. Not through rituals, not through bagels and lox, not just for our own people, but to the whole world. The message of the Messiah.

2

Guideposts

"If you search there for the Lord your God, you will find Him, if only you seek Him with all your heart and soul" (Deut. 4:29).

I was born in a small town in New Hampshire. Later our family moved to a larger community in Massachusetts. When I enrolled in college in Boston, I faced the challenges of the big city. Now I live on a 40-acre homestead in a clearing on a mountainside in northwestern Montana, surrounded by forests. No matter where one lives, in order to get around you must rely on markers to find your bearings. They may be street signs, stores, or unusual landmarks that help you know where you are going and how to return.

Our community of Bradford, Massachusetts, had a common—a grassy, fenced-off park—and a white church with a tall steeple on top. When I would walk to school or head to town, I knew I was halfway there when I reached the common. It was a comforting feeling for a little girl surrounded by big houses and noisy streets filled with frighteningly dangerous cars. The park was a place I could recognize.

Here, as an adult, I still look for markers when I hike through the forest. Without them I could easily lose my way and perish, as the wilderness holds many dangers for the novice. My husband, who has been an outfitter and guide, has learned how to navigate through the 50- to 100-foot trees that often obscure his vision. He has learned the secrets of the outdoors through observation and is able to "read" the forest.

His years as a logger felling trees has taught him much about their nature and various needs, such as that of the willow and cedar, which grow best near wet areas—around springs, creek beds, or bottomlands. By knowing the ecosystem in which different species of trees thrive, my husband can pretty much tell whether he is on the north or south slope of a mountainside. He uses nature's guideposts—its markers—to allow him to chart his course.

When he and our children were working on a logging job, he cut the trees and they tossed the limbs into brush piles. "We're going to be cutting white pine today," he'd tell our son and daughter. The kids didn't know one tree from another at the beginning of the summer, but by the job's end they could easily name them all. By looking at the tree, identifying the color and texture of the bark, smelling the cut branches, and studying the needles and cones, they were able to identify which species the tree was. Thereafter, they were able to walk through the forest and know for certain what a white pine tree was by its characteristics.

On occasion I have been lost on the mountainside above our home, not knowing in which direction I should go after entering the tree line. Every path looked like the right one leading back to our place. With darkness approaching, I've had some anxious moments wondering if I'd have to spend the night in the woods with the cougars, coyotes, and grizzly bears.

But knowing that willow trees, with their smooth, white bark and spade-shaped green (or yellow leaves in fall), stand by water, I have often used them as markers when coming off the mountain, because our spring is not far from our clearing. Like slender sentinels, they have saved me from being lost several times.

Signposts, markers, physical characteristics—they are all guides. They tell us a lot, if we pay attention. To negotiate through the labyrinth called life successfully, we need guideposts. Nature has its own set of rules, which, if ignored or violated, can lead to our being lost and destroyed. Throughout the ages, wise men and women have gone before us, learning life's lessons and taking care to preserve this wisdom under inspiration for us in the Bible. So many say that they wish God had provided an instruction book for their parents (or themselves) when they were born. Yet why they so easily dismiss the guideposts and set of instructions for fruitful living that God has actually given them, I do not know.

How many times have you heard someone say that he or she feels lost and is searching for the truth? Many go to psychologists looking for easy answers. Others trek around the world seeking understanding.

I've searched for God in many ways—through prescribed study in temple school as a youngster, in college, and by visiting shuls, synagogues, temples, and churches of every persuasion. Always driven by the desire to learn more, I have never been completely satisfied that any particular path I have chosen would lead me to the *truth*. Yet I've discovered that there are many ways to find the Lord. For me, though, words are my road maps. Words fascinate me, perhaps because I use them a lot. I like to delve beneath the surface to see where they came from and what other meanings they may have—sometimes out of curiosity, but usually to gain greater knowledge. I have often felt as King Solomon did in Ecclesiastes 7:23 when he described his search for wisdom about the secrets of life. He says that the secrets of life are "elusive" and so deep that "who can discover it?" Like so many of us seekers of truth, he set his mind to "studying, exploring and seeking wisdom and the reason of things." And while he did so, he also saw life's evil side, full of "wickedness, stupidity, madness and folly."

But despite his initial premise that all a person's efforts to succeed in life are futile or vanity, Solomon also recognizes that "Wisdom is superior to folly as light is superior to darkness; A wise man has his eyes in his head, Whereas a fool walks in darkness" (Eccl. 2:13, 14).

Life is a mystery, whose secrets God reveals to whom He chooses and in the time frame He selects. The Bible is a compilation of God's message and conversations with humanity. It contains the rules for successful living not only on this earth but gives us specific guidelines as to how we mortals, once we have concluded our physical lives on this planet, can meet our heavenly Father and live forever with Him in peace and harmony.

God gives us a map. Just as the moon and stars have provided travelers with guideposts throughout history, the Bible directs us to eternal life. Let's continue to walk together as we search for clues to unravel the mysteries within the Bible that will lead you to the wisdom and truth you are seeking in your own life. Follow me.

In Search of the Messiah

Maybe as we walk together and identify some of God's street signs, you will find yourself on a familiar path—one that will also lead you to the truth you are seeking for yourself. Come with me as I retrace my steps in search of the Messiah.

3

Which Bible to Use?

When I began my journey in search of the Messiah in the Guidebook—the Scriptures—that God has given us, I used whatever version was close at hand. But as I became more involved, I began to realize that the authors of the various versions translated the language, sentence structure, and even the specific words themselves differently—so much so that the meanings often do not appear to resemble one another. I have found this especially true when cross-referencing scriptures between Jewish translations of the Hebrew Scriptures and the Old Testament of the Christian King James or New International versions.

I began to wonder if the Christian translators had intentionally looked for references that they could consider Messianic prophecies of Jesus in the Hebrew text. Either they weren't there or were only alluded to, or could be seen only if one stretched the imagination. This same feeling held true when I looked to the new Jewish translations of the Hebrew Scriptures. It appeared as if they were downplaying any references to the coming of a Messiah. I felt perplexed, dismayed, and concerned about the validity of any Bible as a true reference.

So which one should we use? Is there any one *true* Bible?

As a youngster I received a Hebrew Bible in Sabbath school as a confirmation present. It had a white satin cover with a pink satin ribbon to mark the pages, but the pages and size of the type were so small that it was difficult to read. I did use it for many years as my only reference, until the 1960s when I took a course in comparative theology at Boston University. Needing a text with larger type, I purchased a copy of the Torah that had just been published by the Jewish Publication Society of Philadelphia.

Now I am working from the *Tanakh*, a translation of the Holy Scriptures also published by the Jewish Publication Society. It contains the most sacred collection of books of the Jewish people, usually referred to as the Holy Scriptures, the Hebrew Canon, or the Hebrew Bible. The word *Tanakh* is made up of the three initials of its major sections, namely the Torah (Pentateuch), the Nevi'im (Prophets), and the Kethuvim (Writings).

The Torah comprises the five books of Moses—Genesis, Exodus, Leviticus, Numbers, and Deuteronomy. It describes God's creation of the universe and follows the lives of the patriarchs Abraham, Isaac, and Jacob, as well as a historic account of the Israelites as slaves in Egypt. After describing the exodus from Egypt led by Moses, it recounts their wanderings in the desert wilderness and the giving of the Ten Commandments to

Moses on Mount Sinai. The Torah also contains the Mosaic law
that covers both social and religious instruction. The Torah ends
with an account of the death of Moses.

The Nevi'im includes books of history from the perspec-
tive of the prophets—the books of Joshua, Judges, Samuel,
and Kings, referred to as the former prophets; Isaiah,
Jeremiah, and Ezekiel, referred to as the latter prophets; and
Hosea, Joel, Amos, Obadiah, Jonah, Micah, Nahum,
Habakkuk, Zephaniah, Haggai, Zechariah, and Malachi,
brief prophetic books contained on a single scroll and thus
considered together as one book. This second section covers
the history of the Israelites from the time they enter Canaan.

The third section, Kethuvim (the Writings), is divided
into four sections—(1) Psalms, Proverbs, and Job; (2) the
five scrolls of Song of Songs (Solomon), Ruth, Lamentations,
Ecclesiastes, and Esther; (3) Daniel; and (4) Ezra, Nehemiah,
and Chronicles.

Jewish thought ranks them in order of importance as the
Law, the Prophets, and the Writings.

Why are there so many translations of the Bible? Is it because each religious group wanted to include or exclude texts
or superimpose their own version of the ancient writings to
support their own conclusions (Jewish or Christian)? I must
admit when I began switching back and forth from one Bible
translation to another that for a time I thought so. But after
searching for the answers to the reasons for the translations,
I have another opinion.

The greater part of the Old Testament was written in
Hebrew, usually called ancient Hebrew in order to distin-
guish it from Mishnaic and modern Hebrew. Mishnaic
Hebrew is the Hebrew of the Christian Era, an artificially re-

vived language in which the Jewish rabbis wrote their scholarly works and which became the basis for the official language of today's state of Israel. The term "Hebrew language" appears for the first time in the prologue to the apocryphal book of Ecclesiasticus (translated into Greek in 132 B.C.E.*). The Jewish historian Josephus in the first century of the Christian Era mentioned it, as do the later rabbinical writings. The term *Hebrew tongue* used by Luke in Acts 21:40 and 26:14 refers to Aramaic, not to Hebrew. Aramaic was the common language spoken in New Testament times.

Throughout the centuries people have translated the Bible into nearly every language in the world. Parts of it were even incorporated into the Islamic Koran. It is said to be the most widely read book of any ever produced in the world.

The Bibles we use today are not in the original form. Because the ancient Hebrew language had some serious shortcomings—written words consisted only of consonants (no vowels), sentences often were cryptic, and the language contained words that have no exact equivalent in English—it is not possible to translate Hebrew into the English language word-for-word. The Jews first made paraphrases into Aramaic, another Semitic language somewhat similar to Hebrew and first adopted as a common language by the Babylonian Jews around 525 B.C.E. It was the language used during the time of Jesus. Aramaic flourished until the seventh century C.E., when Arabic became the language of the Middle East.

The Targum (the Aramaic paraphrase of the Hebrew Scriptures), the Palestinian and Babylonian Talmud, and parts of the books of Daniel and Ezra were either written or translated into different dialects of Aramaic. Also, the Jewish marriage contract (*ketubbah*), the writ of divorcement (*get*), the Jewish doxology (*kaddish*), and the Jewish mystical writings (*kabbalah*) continue to be utilized in Aramaic until the present day.

As you are well aware, language is a living thing. It changes from region to region and era to era in dialect and word usage and meanings. Throughout history the Bible has been a major source of study by theologians who have treated its contents with great respect and considered the message, even the manner in which the words were written, as divinely inspired. Because of the feelings of awe surrounding the Scriptures, people did not undertake their translation lightly.

And because biblical passages, then as now, have spurred scholarly discussion and interpretation, many versions of the Scriptures have been written down through the ages.

For centuries Hebrew scribes copied the original Hebrew text, until the sixth century B.C.E. when a school of Jewish scholars called the Masoretes took over this work. The Masoretes were grammarians who took great pains to check every letter, word, and phrase of the copies they made for accuracy. As we know, even books such as this one printed today need to be proofread before publication to avoid mistakes.

The Jews also translated the Hebrew Bible into Greek. Completed in Alexandria, Egypt, during the reign of Ptolemy Philadelphus (285-246 B.C.E.), it is called the Septuagint, a word meaning "seventy" for the number of scholars legend says worked on it.

The Dead Sea scrolls, discovered by a Bedouin in 1947 at Khirbet Qumran, a few miles from Jericho, are ancient manuscripts dated by experts to a period between the third century B.C.E. and 70 C.E. Made of pieces of leather and sewn together, scribes rolled the books up and stored them in clay jars in caves. These scrolls are of great importance as they are the earliest known Bible manuscripts. Since the caves in which they were found are located in an area where a Jewish sect called the Essenes flourished during the pre-Christian and early Christian eras, some scholars think the Essenes may have written them.

The ancient Jewish authors Philo and Josephus described the Essenes as being groups of pious people who lived in communities of their own, some of them close to the desert. They were said to be vegetarians, doing manual labor, sharing their earnings, eating together, and dressing very simply, usually in white. They washed and bathed frequently, and seemed to know something of the healing power of herbs, thus earning them a reputation as healers. Others regarded them as holy people because of their restricted and secret ways of life, and also because some of them would go out to preach among the people, urging them to mend their ways and to repent before the "great day of judgment."

Since their discovery, religious scholars the world over have awaited the publication of their contents. Only in 1992—45 years after they were unearthed—did copies of all the scrolls become widely available to researchers outside the original study committee.

The King James Version of the Bible was prepared by 54 of the best biblical scholars in Great Britain who convened under the auspices of King James I to prepare an English translation. The scholars divided into six groups—three to work on a translation of the Old Testament and three on the New Testament. The resulting "Authorized Version" appeared in 1611 and became the primary biblical reference until this day. However, because the language has become antiquated, scholars have released other translations in more modern language.

In 1917 the Jewish Publication Society of America produced its first translation of the Hebrew Bible, and English-speaking Jews the world over quickly accepted it. It is still in use today—as is the original King James Version—and some theologians still favor it.

For those of us who simply want to read and understand the Bible in the language we are familiar with today, the Tanakh and either the New King James Version or the New International Version of the Bible may feel more comfortable. They are easier to understand because they have eliminated the "thees" and "thous" no longer in everyday usage. Also, verbs no longer end in "eth" (i.e., speaketh, heareth, doeth). Though to some the Elizabethan language may be more poetic, for most it is archaic and difficult to comprehend. And since the Bible carries an eternal message to humanity, it is best read in the language of today. It makes God's guideposts easier to spot as we search for the Messiah and God's message for us.

I, for one, like to compare language, messages, and styles. So when I read the Bible, I have two in front of me—the Tanakh and the New King James Version. But I also refer to many other versions, including *The Living Bible*, a paraphrase in contemporary language.

I honestly believe that every effort has been made to bring to us the true meaning of the ancient words of the patriarchs and prophets in these Bible translations. And I am eagerly awaiting the release of the English translations of the Dead Sea scrolls. They are time capsules that survived 2,000 years in the desert—hidden away to be discovered, I believe, at a time appointed by God. The passage from Daniel 12:4 comes to mind when I think of the scrolls. "But you, Daniel, keep the words secret, and seal the book until the time of the end. Many will range far and wide and knowledge will increase" (Tanakh).

Archaeologists have found every book of the Hebrew Bible (Old Testament) among the scrolls except that of Esther, and researchers were surprised to find few variations between the scrolls and the text most Bibles were translated from until recently. That's very reassuring to me. It reinforces my belief that the Bible is true, passed down from generation to generation so that each of us will have an opportunity to study the Scriptures and learn what God has to say to us.

Please join me in my study. Follow along with me as I retrace my search for the Messiah.

---

*B.C.E. and C.E. are abbreviations that stand for Before Common Era and Common Era, and designate the time periods Christians call B.C. and A.D. without the Christian connotation.

4

What Is God's Name?

"I am the Lord, that is My name; I will not yield My glory to another, nor My renown to idols" (Isa. 42:8).

What's in a name? How important is it in your life? Does it matter what others call you?

My birth name is Judith Cortell. My surname reflected that I was a child of my father, Ben Cortell. It identified my lineage. In childhood when I was asked my name, people in the community could identify me as coming from my father's family. Who they were, I was also. Whether his reputation was honest or disreputable transferred to me until I became an adult and established my own reputation. My family instilled in me as a youngster that whatever I did reflected on my father's name. He did not want to be dishonored by my actions. "Behave yourself out there in the world," he would

31

tell me. "I don't want my good name ruined."

When I married, I took the last name of my husband, Ben Simonson, and inherited the history of his family, both good and bad. Also, by this time I had established my own reputation or good name. When anyone asked him whom he married, the honor of my family name was added to his.

As a writer I first used my birth name. However, at that time, being identified as a female was a disadvantage. I would submit articles on various subjects, only to have them returned to me from magazine editors with no reason given on the rejection letters. It was obvious from the condition of the manuscripts that nobody had turned the pages. They had simply looked at my name, Judith, and, seeing I was female, rejected them. So I decided on an experiment to see if my suspicions were correct.

I changed my name to Jay Simons on the byline, resubmitted the identical articles to the same magazines that had originally rejected them, and sold them all. They addressed me "Dear Mr. Simons." Since having a supposedly "male-sounding" name opened doors for me, I have used it since with great success. It also helps me distinguish between friends and family members who refer to me as Judy and those with whom I associate in business. When a telephone caller asks for Jay, I go into my office and get ready for business. If they want to speak to Judy, I pull up an easy chair and relax. It's probably my mother, sisters, or old friends on the line. So what is the value of the name? It carries with it connotations of respect and honor, or the opposite, depending upon its historic lineage.

When I changed my name from Judith Cortell to my husband's, did it change the essence of who I am? Yes, in a way.

WHAT IS GOD'S NAME?

Marriage marked a new dimension in my life. It opened new doors for my growth as a person as I became a wife and then a mother. And it introduced me to new experiences — new knowledge. In that way, I suppose that changing my name did transform who I was.

Each of us needs these street signs — labels — to help us through the maze we call life. How odd it would be if we had no names at all. I believe it would be totally impossible to communicate information to one another.

How would we refer to each other without using proper nouns or even adjectives? Look at me — I am my parents' second daughter. They have two other girls. How could they speak to us to make us understand without calling us by name. Even if they said "Hey, you!" and pointed to one of us with their finger, they are still making a distinction. They could use the title "Daughter No. 2," and people might know whom they were speaking about, but it is far less complicated to give us names.

I remember people calling me Blondie, towhead, and little girl. Each adjective described a physical characteristic. People got a general idea of whom they were talking about by such generalities, but it was not until someone said my full name — my proper name, Judith Marlene Cortell — that the listener would say, "Oh, yes, now I know whom you have in mind."

The same principle applies to God.

I've read the Bible through many times — sometimes just to have accomplished it, other times because of school assignments. But it wasn't until several years ago, when I was searching the Scriptures for specific verses, that I discovered that the patriarchs, prophets, and even God Himself thought that the name by which others called Him was important. I began to notice that the word "name" came up quite frequently. It occurs 928 times in 832 verses of the Bible. I wondered why. So I began to jot down how often, when, where, and why God or the prophets made a specific issue of what God was going to be called in the Scriptures. You'd be amazed once you become aware just how often the phrases "in His name," "in the name of YHWH," "the Lord," etc., occurs. I was discovering one of the guideposts on the trail to the Messiah.

Right from the beginning of the Bible, in Genesis, you can tell that to call a person, place, or thing by its proper name is crucial. And as we go along, you'll see that the different names attributed to God are markers, guideposts, and characteristics, just as the trees in the forest are to me and my family. These markers have fascinated me with what they say about God, and I hope they will fascinate you too.

Let's look, for example, at the story of Creation in the first book of the Bible, Genesis. In Chapter 1 God created light and darkness, the sky and the ocean, dry land, trees, vegetation, stars, the sun and the moon, and all the living creatures of the sea, the air, and the land. That set the stage for His next creation—humanity—to whom He gave dominion over all living things. At that time, the Bible tells us, God called the light, Day, and darkness, Night. He name the sky, the dry land, Earth, and the water, the seas. But He did not name any of the creatures He had created. That honor He gave to man.

After He formed them, He brought them to the first man and waited to see what he would call them. He didn't tell him what the creatures were—He gave him a free rein: ". . . whatever the man called each living creature, that would be its name."

Following each act of creation, Scripture quotes God as

saying that He realized it was good. But when He saw that the man was alone—without a mate—He cast a deep sleep to come upon the man, and while he was sleeping, God removed one of the man's ribs and created for him a female, "a fitting helper."

When He brought her to the man, it deeply moved the first human being. He said,

> "This one at last
> Is bone of my bones
> And flesh of my flesh.
> This one shall be called Woman,
> For from man was she taken" (Gen. 2:23).

It is interesting to note that the next verse refers to the marriage of man and woman as becoming "of one flesh."

"Hence a man leaves his father and mother and clings to his wife, so that they become one flesh."

God gave Adam, the first human being, the exciting opportunity to name each living creature. It was an honor and an awesome responsibility. But does it matter to me that I now know that it was Adam who named the animals and not God? Does it change anything? Maybe not—they are still giraffes, camels, elephants, cows, horses, and pelicans. But isn't it nicer knowing that God had that much trust, love, and respect in His own creation—Adam—to give him that honor? And because Adam named each creature, each of us is able to differentiate in our mind's eyes exactly which animal a person is talking about when they use the proper name for it. When I say the word horse, you don't envision an elephant, do you?

Even the name of the first man—Adam—comes from the Hebrew word *'adamah*, because "the Lord God formed man from the dust of the earth" (Gen. 2:7). *'Adamah* means earth.

But what about God? When you read or say the word *God*, what comes to your mind? What image forms before your eyes? If you are Christian, is it Jesus? How about Allah if you are a Muslim? Maybe Vishnu or Siva if you are a Hindu. What image does the name Buddha bring to mind? Let's give Jehovah a try if you are a Jehovah's Witness, or Adonai if you are of Jewish origin. And we've only scratched the surface. For most, the word *God* means a supreme being — the Creator of the universe. But as you can see, for us to communicate with one another we have to establish some ground rules to know whom we are talking about. I believe it is with this very purpose in mind that the heavenly Father established a specific name by which we shall call Him. The word *God* isn't enough. So does God have a name?

Many have asked that question down through the ages, and it is one that has led me on my journey through the Holy Scriptures. It is a trip that has brought me out of darkness into spiritual light, even though it has taken many unexpected turns. I'd like to share it with you and hope you find it as fascinating and inspiring as I have.

We must remember that even during humanity's early history people worshiped and served many gods. You can still find such worship today throughout the world. It was the Hebrews (Jews) who first introduced the belief that there was only one God. And it was through this God and His power that the salvation of humanity and the opportunity to participate in an afterlife (heaven) was to be assured. So it was of prime importance to give Him a name that would identify who He is as opposed to the many other gods that people worshiped at the time. By looking at what He calls Himself, or how the patriarchs and prophets refer to Him, we will establish and define

His character, influence, and power over humanity.

Let's look at the scripture we have just quoted. In some places it simply calls Him God. In others the word LORD (in all capital letters) precedes God. Does that matter? I wondered. It seemed as though there was something more to this than just the spelling of the name.

As I began my studies I realized that His name is more than a way to address Him or tell Him apart from others in the Holy Scriptures, though the need to differentiate between the Eternal God and false gods is crucial. As we become more involved in finding out who God is, how He is perceived, and the names He goes by, we will see that they not only express His character but also distinguish Him and His relationship to us and to His Son—a fact that becomes very important in our search for God and the Messiah foretold in the Scriptures.

Let's examine Exodus 34:5-7: "The Lord came down in a cloud; He stood with him there, and proclaimed the name Lord. The Lord passed before him and proclaimed: 'The Lord! the Lord! a God compassionate and gracious, slow to anger, abounding in kindness and faithfulness, extending kindness to the thousandth generation, forgiving iniquity, transgression, and sin; yet He does not remit all punishment, but visits the iniquity of parents upon children and children's children, upon the third and fourth generations" (Tanakh).

But is this His real, true, and only name? What do the Scriptures say about His name?

The angels praise His name saying, "Holy, holy, holy! The Lord of Hosts!" in Isaiah 6:3. The word "holy" also appears in Isaiah 57:15 to describe God's character. Speaking about God's name, Nehemiah 9:5 calls it "glorious." Psalm 148:13 describes it as "excellent," and Psalm 111:9 says His name is "holy and reverenced." So now we know that when we speak of God, not only is He said to be holy but His name is also holy.

In Deuteronomy 21:5 we see that God chose the Hebrew priests to minister to Him and to pronounce blessings in the name of the Lord. Deuteronomy 26:2 relates that God told Moses to "go to the place where the Lord your God will choose to establish His name." In Deuteronomy 28:58 God warns Moses that if he fails to observe "all the terms of this Teaching that are written in this book, to reverence this honored and awesome Name, the Lord your God, the Lord will inflict extraordinary plagues" upon him and his descendants. Does that sound as if He really means that His name has a special significance? I believe so. Throughout the Scriptures, God has a definite reason for establishing His name, because He is looking for a people—a nation of priests—to represent Him and to be called by His name.

In 1 Kings 18 the prophet Elijah challenges King Ahab to test the power of his gods against the God of heaven, the God of Israel. He told him to summon all of Israel to join him at Mount Carmel along with 450 prophets of Baal and the 400 prophets of the groves.

When they arrive, he says: "If the Lord is God, follow Him; but if Baal, then follow him" (verse 21, NKJV). Then he told the prophets of Baal to invoke their god by name, and he in turn would call upon the Lord by name. He said, "The god who answers by fire, He is God" (verse 24, NKJV).

When Elijah invoked God's name, he said: "O Lord, God of Abraham, Isaac, and Israel! Let it be known today that You are God in Israel and that I am Your servant, and that I have done all these things at Your bidding. Answer me, O

WHAT IS GOD'S NAME?

Lord, answer me, that this people may know that You, O Lord, are God" (verses 36, 37).

So by what name was He called?

Some believe that the word YHWH, formed by four Hebrew consonants (called the tetragrammaton) and often considered to be the true name of God, is so holy that the word is forbidden to be pronounced except by the high priest in the Holy of Holies on Yom Kippur. Wherever it appears in the Bible or elsewhere, they pronounced it Adonai and reverently referred to it in Hebrew as the *Shem ha-Meforash* (ineffable name). The word is formed from the Hebrew consonant letters Yod, He, Vav, and He. Its pronunciation is uncertain, though modern scholars suggest that its original pronunciation was "Yahveh." The Masoretes, early Jewish scholars, took the vowel signs from the word *'adonai* and placed them in the margins so that when the rabbis read the word YHWH, which could not be pronounced, it became Yahveh or Yahweh. In the early days of the Reformation, when Christians learned to use the Hebrew Bible, they transliterated the holy name of God as "Jehovah." It is also translated "Lord," or "God."

The Jews regarded the tetragrammaton as extremely sacred. During the last three centuries B.C.E., they began to fear to utter it aloud or even write it down fully because God's power was omniscient, overwhelming, and awe-inspiring. That is why you sometimes see even the word "God" written "G-d" in modern Jewish publications. Reverence, awe, and fear surround the name of God—so much so that Jews even have a special storeroom for Hebrew books no longer physically fit for use but which cannot be destroyed because they contain the name of God. These materials are called *Shemot* (names), and it is an old custom to bury *Shemot* with the bodies of pious Jews. The Hebrew term for this special hiding place is *Genizah*, and it is usually the attic or cellar of a synagogue.

Because the name of God is so important to our heavenly Father, when He inscribed the Ten Commandments on the tablets of stone, one of those rules for living declared: "You shall not swear falsely by the name of the Lord your God" (Ex. 20:7).

But which name does He mean? The God of heaven, the true God that the ancient Hebrews recognized, actually revealed Himself by several different names throughout the centuries. The Hebrew Bible associates many names and titles with God. I'd like to share with you some of the other names that also refer to God.

Exodus 6:2, 3, says: "God spoke to Moses and said to him, 'I am the Lord. I appeared to Abraham, Isaac, and Jacob as *El Shaddai,* but I did not make myself known to them by my name YHWH."

As you can see, following the naming of God can get confusing. What does it mean? Are we just splitting hairs? Or are the different names adjectives, definitions of various aspects of God's abilities, personality, character, and relationship with His creation?

Could it be like the name that my parents bestowed upon me at birth—my formal, recorded name on my birth certificate? Or my Hebrew name, Yehuda Leah, that appears on my confirmation and bas mitzvah certificates as well as on my Jewish wedding certificate? Or the two other names that different people refer to me by—Judy or Jay? All are names that I recognize and answer to, depending upon who is calling me and for what purpose or relationship. That sounded logical to me, but I wanted to discover for myself by following the trail of names left as clues in the Holy Scriptures and by seeking the meanings of the Hebrew words attributed to Him.

Join me as we look at what the ancient Hebrews called their God.

YAHWEH or JEHOVAH: One Who Is Who He Is (The Living God)

This name, incorrectly translated in English as Jehovah, is formed by two tenses of the Hebrew verb *havah*, "to be," and means "one who is who he is." "In appearance, YHWH is the third person singular imperfect 'kal' of the verb (to be), meaning, therefore, 'He is,' or 'He will be,' or perhaps, 'He lives,' the root idea of the word being, probably, 'to blow, to breathe,' and hence, 'to live,' which carries through with the meaning of the name given in Ex. 3:14, where God is represented as speaking, and hence as using the first person — 'I am.' That meaning one who is self-existing, self-sufficient, or 'He who lives.'

"The idea of being life-giving has been connected with YHWH since ancient times. He is the living God, as contrasted with the lifeless gods of the heathen, and He is the source and author of life. No other god makes that claim."[1]

This same form appears in Exodus 3:13-15, where Moses has been told by God to go to the Egyptian Pharaoh and free His people, the Israelites, from slavery in Egypt. The command dumbfounded Moses. He felt unworthy to fulfill it. Moses felt that the Pharaoh would not believe that his mission came directly from the God of Israel. But God assured him, saying, "I will be with you; that will be the sign that it was I who sent you."

But when Moses asked God what to say to the Israelites

when they asked him the name of the God who sent him to them, God replied, "Ehyeh-Asher-Ehyeh." (The meaning of the Hebrew in this phrase has been variously translated as: "I Am That I Am"; "I Am Who I Am"; or "I Will Be What I Will Be.") He continued, "Thus shall you say to the Israelites, 'Ehyeh sent me to you.' And God said further to Moses, 'Thus shall you speak to the Israelites: The Lord [YHWH], the God of your fathers, the God of Abraham, the God of Isaac, and the God of Jacob, has sent me to you: This shall be My name forever, this My appellation for all eternity.'"

"This shall be My name forever." That sounds pretty clear to me. Doesn't it to you? "This My appellation for all eternity." We'd better start learning it, don't you think? Appellation — designation, title. To me this is flag, a guidepost.

God is quite clear about what His name was, is, and will be. So why did the ancient Hebrews need to use other names to address or refer to Him? As we look at these names and at their uses in Scripture, it appears to me that God is making it perfectly clear to man who He is so there will not be any question about Him. He is an ever-living God, a here-and-now God who spans all generations past, present, and future. He is not a finite object, such as an idol of wood, stone, metal, or plastic.

In Isaiah, through whom God has written letters to us, He says, "I am the first and I am the last and there is no god but Me" (Isa. 44:6). I'd say there's no question there, don't you agree? This chapter contains so much good information. Please read it for yourself. God gets pretty specific how He feels about idols and those who craft them.

Here are some other references in Scripture that speak to this present tense, describing Him as a "living" God.

"I am the first and I am the last" (Isa. 44:6).

WHAT IS GOD'S NAME?

"I am God, your God!" (Ps. 50:7, NKJV).

What kind of God is He, this One who is with us? Fundamental Judaism says "that God exists, that He is pure spirit, that He is eternal, good, holy, true, faithful, just, loving, and full of compassion. . . . He is the Author of the laws of nature as well as of ethics and morality. He is all-powerful, all-knowing, and both love and justice are the essence of His being. God's providence is over all His creatures. He is a person in the sense that He hears prayer and reveals His will to man."[2]

What is this YHWH like? He is a God of real, deep, love and affection. He cares greatly for all of His creation. In a way, God seems like a pushover because He is so forgiving of man's sins. But justice always tempers YHWH's love. Each of us knows what justice is. That's when the bad guy gets what's coming to him. Justice is why cowboy movies in the 1950s and 1960s were so popular. Everything was cut and dried. The bad guys got punished in the end.

God's attributes are clearly described in Exodus 34:6, 7: "A God compassionate and gracious, slow to anger, abounding in kindness and faithfulness, extending kindness to the thousandth generation, forgiving iniquity, transgression, and sin; yet He does not remit all punishment, but visits the iniquity of parents upon children and children's children, upon the third and fourth generations."

According to the Scripture, God (YHWH) will do everything possible to save human beings from destruction, but if they reject His plan of salvation or decide they want to be saved on their own terms, then He has no other option but to destroy them in order to rid the universe of sin.

Isaiah 42:8 presents Him as the eternal one. "I am the

LORD: that is my name." The prophet Jeremiah speaks of Him "whose name is Lord" (Jer. 33:2).

He is *Yah*, a short, poetic form of YHWH: "Sing to God [Elohim], chant hymns to His name; extol Him who rides the clouds; the Lord [Yah] is His name" (Ps. 68:5; see also Isa. 38:11).

Scripture also uses combinations of names, such as 'Adonai Yahweh (Lord God) in Ezekiel 36:23. "I will sanctify My great name. . . . And the nations shall know that I am the Lord [YHWH]—declares the Lord God ['Adonai YHWH]."

In Genesis 2:7 He is Yahweh 'Elohim (Lord God). Psalm 109:21 calls Him Yahweh 'Adonai (God the Lord).

ADONAI (Lord)

The Hebrew word *'Adonai* signifies "lord," "master," and "ownership." It is a term God's servants seemed to use when they doubted or misunderstood God's instructions, such as in Genesis 15:2: "But Abram said, 'O Lord God, what can You ['Adonai] give me, seeing that I shall die childless?'"

And in Exodus 4:10-12 when Moses humbly spoke to God, he used the 'Adonai form: "But Moses said to the Lord, 'Please, O Lord ['Adonai], I have never been a man of words."

Gideon spoke to God in Judges 6:15: "'Please, my lord ['adonai], how can I deliver Israel? Why, my clan is the humblest in Manasseh, and I am the youngest in my father's household."

Adonai means God, but in the context of a master/servant relationship. "O Lord ['Adonai], hear! O Lord ['Adonai], forgive! . . . For Your name is attached to Your city and Your people" (Dan. 9:19).

What Is God's Name?

ELOHIM (Gods)

Though we have seen that the God of heaven has said His name is YHWH, and whenHe appeared to Moses it was as "Ehyeh-Asher-Ehyeh," the Hebrew word *Elohim* (gods) is the first name used in the Bible to refer to God the Creator in Genesis 1. When God established the heavens and the earth, He did it by saying, "Let there be". . . light, sky, earth, the seas, and all the vegetation and animals. But when it came to creating man, He declared, "Let us make man in our image, after our likeness" (Gen. 1:26).

Who was there with YHWH during the creation? Other gods? Angels? Does God have a family in eternity?

The singular or plural nature of God is of great importance. It is a marker—a signpost—in our search for the Messiah. We will discuss this in greater detail in the chapter on the unity of God.

He is 'Elohim (the Great Ones). "God ['Elohim] . . . said to David and to his son Solomon, 'In this House and in Jerusalem, which I chose out of all the tribes of Israel, I will establish My name forever'" (2 Chron. 33:7). Earlier Solomon had said: "See, I intend to build a House for the name of the Lord my God. . . . The House that I intend to build will be great, inasmuch as our God ['Elohim] is greater than all gods" (2 Chron. 2:3, 4).

EL SHADDAI

Have you heard the beautiful song "El Shaddai"? It has a haunting melody, one that arouses a love for our heavenly Father. What does it mean, and where does it come from in the Bible?

It is a name whose meaning still confuses biblical scholars.

Broken down into its parts, *El* means "Almighty" and *Shad* means "woman's breast." Others have seen it as an allusion to God of the mountains. Translators usually render the phrase "God Almighty."

Speaking of his son Joseph, Jacob said, "The God of your father who helps you, and Shaddai who blesses you with blessings of heaven above, blessings of the deep that couches below, blessings of the breast and womb" (Gen. 49:25). The name seems to represent God's concern for us.

"When Abram was ninety-nine years old, the Lord appeared to Abram and said to him, 'I am El Shaddai. Walk in My ways and be blameless. I will establish My covenant between Me and you, and I will make you exceedingly numerous'" (Gen. 17:1, 2).

God spoke to Moses and said to him, "I am the Lord. I appeared to Abraham, Isaac, and Jacob as El Shaddai, but I did not make Myself known to them by My name YHWH. I also established My covenant with them, to give them the land of Canaan, the land in which they lived as sojourners."

EL ELYON — The Most High (Majesty, Kingship)

Bible references using this title for God do so in the context of His being the King of kings. In Genesis 14:17-21 Moses describes a battle between several invading kings and the rulers of Sodom and Gomorrah. In the conflict Abram's nephew, Lot, gets taken captive. Abram pursued the armies and was able to release Lot, his possessions, and people.

When he returned, King Melchizedek of Salem, priest of El 'Elyon (God Most High), addressed Abram and referred to him also as a believer in the God Most High and used the term El 'Elyon.

WHAT IS GOD'S NAME?

When Abram replied, he invoked God not only as El 'Elyon, but also Lord and Creator of heaven and Earth.

I see the ultimate kingship of God most clearly in the story of King Nebuchadnezzar in Daniel 4. Nebuchadnezzar captured Daniel and three friends and took them to Babylon. These young men continued to be true to Yahweh, observing His commandments and obeying the Mosaic dietary laws. While the others ate food sacrificed to idols and drank the king's wine, Daniel and the other three did not. And they thrived on their simple vegetarian diet. Whenever the king needed the answer to a question that required wisdom and understanding, he discovered their answers to be far superior to those of the court magicians and exorcists in his land.

In chapter 3 the Babylonian king had a dream that caused him great anxiety. He demanded that his magicians and wise men explain the dream, and if they could not, they would be "torn limb from limb" and their possessions confiscated. The men could not.

But the God of heaven came to Daniel in a vision, making the dream clear. Daniel praised God and thanked Him for revealing the dream and thus saving his and the other three Judaean exiles' lives. When he explained the dream to Nebuchadnezzar, he told him that he had seen a great statue. The head of gold represented the Babylonian king. (The dream appears in Dan. 2:31-36.)

Daniel spoke of Babylon's fall and subsequent takeover by other, lesser kingdoms. But he also told Nebuchadnezzar that the God of heaven would establish another kingdom that shall never be destroyed or transferred to another people.

Reading this passage, it would appear that King Nebuchadnezzar received the same kind of authority that

God gave Adam in Genesis—dominion over all living creatures. I'm sure that symbolism wasn't lost on him—it probably went to his head. Eventually the king constructed the enormous statue that had appeared to him in the dream and then commanded that people from every land worship it.

When Daniel's friends refused to do so, the king had the three men thrown into a hot furnace. But when Nebuchadnezzar looked into it, expecting to see them burned to a crisp, he saw instead four men walking around in the furnace, untouched by the flames. The fourth was a mystery. Scripture describes him as a "divine being." Who could that have been? God? An angel? Jesus Christ, as Christian theologians say?

Overwhelmed by the incident, the king ordered that anyone who "blasphemed the God of Shadrach, Mesach and Abednego would be torn limb from limb and his house confiscated, for there is no other God who is able to save in this way."

Sadly, though, Nebuchadnezzar forgot the experience. Like the Pharaoh in Egypt, it took a lesson from God that touched him personally to get the point across.

And God did this again in another dream. The king once again demanded an explanation of it from his wise men and from Daniel, whom he renamed Belteshazzar after the king's god. Daniel told Nebuchadnezzar that the dream again involved him. He saw Nebuchadnezzar, represented by a tall strong tree, being cut down and destroyed. The stump would be encircled in chains of iron and bronze. God would reduce the king to the level of the animals in the field for seven years.

The reason for this punishment, Daniel explained, was that Nebuchadnezzar needed to know once and for all that God is El 'Elyon—the Most High and sovereign over all humanity. The reason the stump and the roots were left in the ground was so that the kingdom would remain his until he acknowledged that "heaven is sovereign."

The dream came true. Nebuchadnezzar ate grass like the cattle and it rained all over him. His hair grew long and shaggy "like eagle's feathers" and his nails "like [the talons] of birds."

After the seven years had passed, Nebuchadnezzar saw the light and acknowledged "the Most High" and "the everliving one." He learned that it is God who has dominion over all life and that it is He who decides the fate of all on earth. No one can "stay His hand."

He declared, "So I, Nebuchadnezzar, praise, exalt and glorify the King of Heaven, all of whose works are just and whose ways are right and who is able to humble those who behave arrogantly."

He got the point. Have we? I think many heads of state, heads of families, and employers would do well to study this experience. Each of us can learn something when it comes to abuse of position and power.

EL OLAM—The Everlasting God

Psalm 90:1, 2: "O Lord, You have been our refuge in every generation. Before the mountains came into being, before You brought forth the earth and the world, from eternity to eternity You are God."

EL ROI—The God Who Sees

This is a story that has a message for us today. It is a perfect example of what happens to us when we do not trust God's promises, or when we tire of waiting for Him to work things out for us, and we decide to do it ourselves. Sarai's impatience and the jealousy that resulted because of her actions has altered the history of the world.

God had promised Abram, as he was first known, that he would be the father of nations. His descendants would be as numerous as the stars in the sky. But his wife, Sarai, had been unable to conceive. She convinced Abram to have sex with her Egyptian servant, Hagar, so Sarai could have a child to raise.

He did that, and when Hagar became pregnant, she felt superior to Sarai, who suddenly began acting as the injured party, blaming Abram for her humiliation. She told him to send Hagar away. Abram advised Sarai to deal with the problem herself. But Sarai treated Hagar harshly and she ran away into the wilderness.

While she was lying by a spring, an angel of the Lord came to her and called her by name, asking where she had come from and where she was going. When she explained that she was running away from Sarai and why, the angel advised her to return to Sarai and submit to her treatment.

Hagar called the Lord El-roi, the God who sees. Genesis 16:13 translates it as "Have I not gone on seeing after He saw me." I saw this passage in several ways. Hagar says that she still has her sight after having seen God (not an angel), whose brilliance other biblical passages have described as "blinding." Since Hagar still had her sight, she considered it a miracle to have seen God face-to-face and not become blind. I also see the implied message that God cares enough for Hagar to watch over her upon her return to Sarai—implying that He will protect her.

God did not leave Hagar without hope and guidance. The angel told her that she would have Abram's baby and it would be a son. That her offspring would be "too many to count." The angel said that she should name him Ishmael [God heeds], because God "took heed of her suffering."

This child of the illicit relationship, however, would not be the one who would bring a blessing to Abram and Sarai. He was born when Abram was 86 years old. And as prophesied, Ishmael would be "a wild ass of a man" with "his hand against everyone" and "everyone's hand against him" (Gen. 16:11).

JEHOVAH SABAOTH—"Lord of Hosts"

This is a term Bible writers used during times of crisis, failure, or defeat. It appears 80 times in the book of Jeremiah, 14 times in two short chapters of Haggai, nearly 50 times in Zechariah, and 25 times in Malachi. It is a name that I believe means Heavenly commander of overwhelming power and forces. Commander in Chief of armies.

David used it as he fought the Philistine giant: "You come against me with sword and spear and javelin; but I come against you in the name of the Lord of Hosts [Jehovah Sabaoth], the God of the ranks of Israel, whom you have defied" (1 Sam. 17:45).

When the hosts of Assyria threatened to destroy Israel, Isaiah saw a greater vision of Jehovah Sabaoth. "In the year that King Uzziah died, I beheld my Lord seated on a high and lofty throne. . . . Seraphs stood in attendance on Him. . . . And one would call to the other, 'Holy, holy, holy! The Lord of Hosts! His presence fills all the earth'" (Isa. 6:1-3).

God's people could call upon Jehovah Sabaoth in times of trouble. "God is our refuge and stronghold, a help in trouble, very near. Therefore we are not afraid though the earth reels, though mountains topple into the sea—its waters rage and foam; in its swell mountains quake. . . . The Lord of Hosts is with us; the God of Jacob is our haven" (Ps. 46:1-12).

YHWH was the name by which the people of the Old Testament knew God as they faithfully served Him. Though Israel's neighbors had many gods, none of them apparently used YHWH to refer to their gods. However, they did use *'el*, *elah*, *'elohim*, and *'adon* to refer to their deities. And the Hebrews would employ *'elohim* when referring to pagan deities (2 Chron. 32:13). In the Hebrew Bible YHWH appears 5,989 times in its full form. "The names used for God were significant. Elohim was the generic term for Deity. Jahweh (Yahweh) the personal name of the God of Israel."[3]

So we see that it was important for everyone to know exactly to which god the patriarchs and prophets were referring when they made pronouncements in His name.

So what is the meaning of the name YHWH? It implies that He is the giver of life, the living God, the all-knowing, all encompassing God of all. The God of Abraham, Isaac, and Jacob—the God of Israel throughout the ages. The one who was, is, and ever will be.

"Sing to God, chant hymns to His name; extol Him who rides the clouds; the Lord [Yah] is His name. Exult in His presence" (Ps. 68:5). "Hallelujah" is a Hebrew word meaning "Praise Yah."

"It was the great prophets who put into the name Yahweh its universal significance, and who saw in the God of Israel the God of the whole universe . . . The more the prophets were brought to realize what God was in Himself, the more they realized that ultimately everything went back to Him. Nothing could be independent of the power and purpose of the everlasting God—'the Eternal.'"[4]

It fascinated me as I traced the various names of God in the Bible and in other reference material. As a Jew I found many of the names familiar to me. I'd grown up hearing them in temple services, sung them many times, and repeated them in prayers. Although I had never heard Yahweh pronounced in the synagogue, I easily recall the various forms of 'Adonai.

I first learned the word, Yahweh, in college classes, but it was not until I began my search for the Messiah that I became aware of and decided to look more closely at the names attributed to God in the Scriptures. And more than that, I wanted to discover if there was something specific being said to us by these names and those of His Son and their relationship to each other and to us.

I feel that the various names by which God revealed Himself to man in biblical times show His desire to be close to us in a parent-child relationship. He wants us to know Him and to be assured that He will always be with us. If we will put our hopes and fears in His hands, He will help us. His love endures forever throughout all generations.

But to know God's name(s) is just the first step . . . the beginning in our search. We need to look for the answer to the question in Proverbs 30:4, which asks, "What is His name, and what is His Son's name, if you know?" (NKJV). Let's look for the answer in the next chapter.

---

[1] *The Jewish Encyclopedia*, vol. 9, p. 160.
[2] *The New Jewish Encyclopedia*, p. 168.
[3] *The New Jewish Encyclopedia*, vol. 6, p. 253.
[4] *Harper's Bible Dictionary* (1956), p. 230.

5

The Son's Name

"What is His name, and what is His Son's name, if you know?" (Prov. 30:4, NKJV).

Scripture constantly identifies people as being "the son of . . ." for the purpose of differentiating between individuals who hold common first names. The biblical writers gave not only the parentage but also in some cases the time in which the person lived. For example, the book of Isaiah begins with the words "The prophecies of Isaiah son of Amoz, who prophesied concerning Judah and Jerusalem in the reigns of Uzziah, Jotham, Ahaz, and Hezekiah, kings of Judah" (Isa. 1:1).

So in Proverbs 30 when Agur asks the identity of the name of God's Son, I listen.

Does God have a Son? I wanted to know, just as Agur did. Many have been referred to as the Son of God. And the

Christian New Testament constantly describes Jesus Christ as the "only begotten Son of God." But is He? And how can we know for certain? And is Jesus Christ the Messiah whose coming Orthodox Jews await when they pray the words in the "Thirteen Principles of the Faith": "I believe with perfect faith in the coming of the Messiah, and, though He tarry, I will wait daily for His coming"?

To have a child to carry on your name and your work has been high on the list of traditional values. When my husband and I found out we were going to have a baby, we both wanted that firstborn to be a son. When he was born, we wanted to give him a name that would carry on his heritage and genealogy. Since my husband's name is Ben and both his father's and grandfather's names also were Ben, plus my own father's name was Ben, the choice was clear. The fourth-generation son would be named Ben. To be named not only for his father but with his father's surname would identify this child as coming from a long line of Ben Simonsons.

Jewish tradition holds that a newborn child should be named for an honored dead person. My husband's father was dead at that time, though my own father was living. In some way I felt it an honor to my father to name our son after him as well. (Jewish tradition, however, discourages naming children after the living to avoid confusion between parent and child. And such confusion does occur. When I want my husband and call for him by name, both answer. Or when someone telephones our house, we have to ask if they want to speak with Ben the father or Ben the son. So Jewish tradition rests upon the wisdom of experience. It should be heeded.)

God the Creator, our heavenly Father, was protective of His name. It is holy, as we have seen in the previous chapter.

He did not want any confusion to occur as to who He was. People have served many gods throughout time—gods in the shape of creatures He had created, or gods in human form fashioned from wood, silver, and gold. Throughout Scripture it is obvious that He didn't want to be included with the others.

Many cultures refer to the earth as Mother, for from her womb comes the food that sustains life. But in Genesis 2:7 it is stated that God created humanity from the dust of the earth. Is Adam, then, the son of God? Let's look at what the Scriptures say.

"And God said, 'Let us make man in our image, after our likeness'" (Gen. 12:6). The original Hebrew uses the plural: "'Let *us* make man in *our* image, after *our* likeness.'" What does "our likeness" mean? To whom was God speaking when He said that? Is there an error in the translation? Could there have been more gods with YHWH when He made His pronouncement? A family of gods, perhaps? Remember from chapter 1 we saw that YHWH was not the term used in this section of Genesis. Rather, it was *'Elohim*—a term meaning Gods, but not the name He preferred to use for Himself. So who was with Him, when He established the earth? We'll discuss this in detail in a later chapter.

The first human being on earth was Adam. Then, seeing that Adam was lonely and that there was no suitable mate for him, God created Eve (in Hebrew, *Havvah*, "life-bearer") from Adam's rib. (This creation from his flesh is such a beautiful symbolism of the oneness of man and woman, yet how often the importance of its meaning is lost on modern-day couples.) Together the first couple became the parents of all succeeding generations. We ask, then, was Adam God's Son? If God made him in His image and likeness, would that not lead us to believe so? And then is Eve God's daughter? These are good questions.

But in other verses in the Bible we find references to "divine beings." Genesis 6:1-4, for example, speaks of "divine beings" consorting with humans:

"When men began to increase on earth and daughters were born to them, the divine beings saw how beautiful the daughters of man were and took wives from among those that pleased them. — The Lord said, 'My breath shall not abide in man forever, since he too is flesh; let the days allowed him be one hundred and twenty years.' — It was then, and later too, that the Nephilim appeared on earth — when the divine beings cohabited with the daughters of men, who bore them offspring. They were the heroes of old, the men of renown."

Some translations render "divine beings" as "the sons of God." The phrase has been interpreted in various ways. Ancient Jewish commentators thought these "sons" were angels, comparing them with the "divine beings" of Job 1:6; 2:1; 38:7. The "sons of God" have also been interpreted as the descendants of Seth and the daughters of the unbelieving Cainites. "Son of God" was also a title commonly used when speaking about Israelite and Egyptian kings and Roman emperors.

Though we may speculate about the mention of "divine beings" in other chapters, we see the first clear definition of who exactly is God's Son in Exodus 4:22. God instructs Moses to return to Egypt and perform certain miracles. "Then you shall say to Pharaoh, 'Thus says the Lord: *Israel is My first-born son.* I have said to you, "Let My son go, that he may worship Me," yet you refuse to let him go. Now I will slay your first-born son.'"

Scripture does not have God calling Adam His son, yet here He speaks of the people of Israel as His firstborn son.

Therefore, it appears that the heavenly Father does not claim the "divine beings" or "sons of God" as His issue.

Nephilim has been translated into the Latin as *gigantes*, from which we derive the English word "giant." In Numbers 13:17 Moses sent men to scout the land of Canaan, telling them to find out what kind of country it was and the strength of the people who dwelled there.

After exploring it for 40 days, they returned to the Israelite camp and reported that the land was indeed flowing with milk and honey, and they returned with some of the first ripe fruit, including a single cluster of grapes so heavy that it took two of them to carry it.

In Numbers 13:30-33 Caleb told the people to be quiet before Moses and encouraged them to attack the Canaanites, saying that he had great faith that they could overcome them and take possession of their land.

But those who had scouted out the territory disagreed, protesting that the enemy was so much bigger and stronger that the Israelites could not possibly attack them and win. "We saw the Nephilim there—the Anakites are part of the Nephilim—and we looked like grasshoppers to ourselves, and so must we have looked to them" (verses 32, 33).

So from reading these passages it becomes clearer that Genesis 6 was referring not to the "sons of God [YHWH]," but of men of such overwhelming size and abilities as to appear like "divine beings."

Throughout Scripture we find great emphasis on documenting genealogy—what we commonly refer to as the "begats." In addition to who begat whom, Genesis preserves data on how many years the patriarchs lived and in many cases their age when their sons and daughters were born.

THE SON'S NAME

As a child and teenager, when I got to these lists in the Bible, I flipped the pages to get past them because to me they were boring, redundant, and served no real purpose. But as I continued to study as an adult, and especially when I became interested in discovering more about the Messiah, I saw that there was a very good reason why Scripture documented lineage.

The great Flood that God sent killed all flesh except Noah, his family, and the creatures on the ark. From his three sons descend the rest of the human race.

We have already seen that God called the nation of Israel as His firstborn son. But that declaration takes place much later, at the time of the Exodus. Noah survived the Flood because he *chose* to follow God—to listen to Him, and to act upon his faith in God's Word. Despite the fact that no one else believed that God would send rain to cover the earth, Noah believed and acted upon that belief. And he remained faithful and believing in God's promise when others fell away. His act of choosing has a direct bearing on what follows.

Remember that God established His covenant between Noah and his offspring to save them in the ark. He said He would maintain His covenant with Noah and his sons forever, that another flood would never again destroy the earth and all living things. The rainbow was God's sign of that covenant.

We'll discuss covenants in detail in a later chapter, but here we'll say only that there are promises between individuals, and that they are also contractual agreements that either party can break.

Now comes the importance of the "begats." They are additional guideposts, or markers, in our search for the Messiah. Many generations down the line of Shem comes a man his parents called Abram, but who God will later name Abraham, the father of the Jewish nation. In Genesis 12:1-3 God called Abram out of his native land to a land that He would show him. God promised him that if he did as he was asked, God would make him "a great nation." He would bless him, make his name great, and help him to be a blessing to others.

Like Noah when he accepted God's challenge, Abram packed up immediately and left, doing as the Lord had told him. He was 75 years old when he departed Haran, where he and his father, Terah, had settled after leaving Ur of the Chaldees. When he and his household arrived in the land of Canaan, Abram passed through it as far as the site of Shechem.

"The Lord appeared to Abram and said, 'I will assign this land to your offspring.' And he built an altar there to the Lord who had appeared to him" (verse 7). Here was another promise God made to Abram, and it gave him hope and courage. After all, the Canaanites held the land solidly. It seemed an impossibility, but Abram believed God and immediately thanked Him by publicly acknowledging His presence—he set up an altar from the stones there and again near Bethel, where he *invoked the Lord by name* (Gen. 12:8).

What name do you think he used? It was *YHWH*. Throughout Scripture, when God speaks, He says, "It was as YHWH that I came to Abraham, Isaac, and Jacob."

Abram was to receive another test of his faith. He was not to remain in Canaan or receive the promise at that time. Instead, he'd have to wait. A famine struck Canaan, and he had to go down to Egypt to survive it. Later he went up into the Negeb.

Unfortunately the land couldn't support the flocks and herds of both Abram and his nephew Lot, and their servants began to bicker and quarrel. So for the sake of harmony, Abram told Lot it would be better if they each went their own way.

Despite his wealth, Abram had no offspring, no son to carry on his lineage, and it vexed him. When God in a vision promised him a great reward, Abram replied: "O Lord God, what can You give me, seeing that I shall die childless. . . . Since You have granted me no offspring, my steward will be my heir." The Lord spoke to him in reply: "'That one shall not be your heir; none but your very own issue shall be your heir.' He took him outside and said, 'Look toward heaven and count the stars, if you are able to count them.' And He added, 'So shall your offspring be.' And because he put his trust in the Lord, He reckoned it to his merit" (Gen. 15:1-6).

Here again Abram chooses to trust and obey God's instructions, despite that to all outward signs the opposite seemed to be true. His was true faith.

Abram and his wife, Sarai, were both old, and Sarai was past the age of childbearing. And though Abram trusted the Lord, his wife didn't share his faith that she would have a child. After all, she and Abram had wanted children all their married life, and she had already passed menopause, so that under all natural circumstances there would be no more opportunities for her to bear children. She became worried. And because she loved her husband and wanted him to have a son, she offered her servant, the Egyptian Hagar, to Abram for a concubine—a substitute, a surrogate mother—so that perhaps through her he would have a chance of producing a son.

It took many more years—when Abram was 99—before that promise of the special child would come true. God came to Abram as El Shaddai and made a covenant with him. Abram would not only father the son he so desperately wanted, but he would become "the father of a multitude of nations" and would bless all the peoples of the earth. His descendants would include kings. The land that Abram was staying in—Canaan—would be his "as an everlasting holding." And God promised to maintain His part of the bargain, the covenant, throughout all generations. He would be God to Abram and his offspring forever.

This is God's part of the bargain. But Abraham also has his promise to make and keep, which God describes to Abram as "Walk in My ways and be blameless." That's what Abraham and his children must do to keep their part of the bargain. He required a physical, external sign from Abram. All males in his family and household—including slaves and outsiders—were to be circumcised.

When God struck His bargain, He did something important—something that only parents do for a child. He gave him a new name, changing it from Abram (the Father is exalted) to Abraham (the father of a multitude). Also He changed Sarai's name to Sarah (princess). I see this renaming of Abram and Sarai as a symbolic act—their new beginning as partners with God in parenting . . . their role in His choice of parents for His Son.

When God made His promise that Abraham and his wife would have a son, Abraham was nearly 100 years of age and Sarah was 90, well beyond the age of childbearing. When he heard God's pronouncement, the old man fell on his face and laughed. Sarah, who was in another room, laughed to herself, too, because she considered the thought preposterous.

Abraham, who acknowledged Ishmael as his son, asked God to bless his son also. God assured Abraham that He would bless Ishmael, and the son would also father many children. But the covenant that He made with Abraham would not pass down through Ishmael's progeny, but through the child of Abraham and Sarah.

God named Abraham's son Isaac, which means "laughter," possibly from the response He received from both Abraham and Sarah when He brought them the good news of the impending birth. Or it would have come from Sarah's words "God has brought me laughter; everyone who hears will laugh with me." The Lord has a sense of humor, too.

Because God needed faithful and trustworthy servants through whom His own Son would be born, God put Abraham through a crucial test. One that He Himself would also experience in generations to come. God told Abraham to take his beloved son Isaac to the land of Moriah and offer him there as a burnt offering on one of the hills that God would point out to him. Can you imagine God asking such a sacrifice from Abraham? Here he had been so faithful, so trustworthy all his life that he had waited until he was 100 years of age before he saw the promise of a son fulfilled. Yet now God was requiring that very son as a sacrifice from him. It seemed preposterous. Yet Abraham followed God's instruction.

After traveling to the place where God told him, he took wood for the burnt offering and put it on his son Isaac. Abraham took the flintstone and the knife, and the two walked together to the top of the mountain. I wonder what was going through Abraham's mind at that moment. Scripture shows us only a calm man. I see no hysteria, no anguish, in these words, only the actions of a deliberate person.

"Then Isaac said to his father Abraham, 'Father!' And he answered, 'Yes, my son.' And he said, 'Here are the firestone and the wood; but where is the sheep for the burnt offering?' And Abraham said, 'God will see to the sheep for His burnt offering, my son.' And the two of them walked on together.

"They arrived at the place of which God had told him. Abraham built an altar there; he laid out the wood; he bound his son Isaac; he laid him on the altar, on top of the wood. And Abraham picked up the knife to slay his son. Then an angel of the Lord called to him from heaven: 'Abraham! Abraham!' And he answered, 'Here I am.' And he said, 'Do not raise your hand against the boy, or do anything to him. For now I know that you fear God, since you have not withheld your son, your favored one, from Me.' When Abraham looked up, his eye fell upon a ram, caught in the thicket by its horns. So Abraham went and took the ram and offered it up as a burnt offering in place of his son. And Abraham named that site Adonai-yireh, whence the present saying, 'On the mount of the Lord there is vision'" (Gen. 22:7-14).

As a result of this supreme test, verses 15-18 announce: "The angel of the Lord called to Abraham a second time from heaven, and said, 'By Myself I swear, the Lord declares: Because you have done this and have not withheld your son, your favored one, I will bestow My blessing upon you and make your descendants as numerous as the stars of heaven and the sands on the seashore; and your descendants shall seize the gates of their foes. All the nations of the earth shall bless themselves by your descendants, because you have obeyed My command.'"

There it is again. Trust and obey, faith and action—choosing to go along with God despite incredible odds. And how did Isaac turn out after all this? Did he follow God? Was he a progenitor of God's son?

When Isaac was 40 years old, he married Rebekah. And she, like his mother, Sarah, was barren. So Isaac pleaded with the Lord on her behalf, and she conceived twins. They struggled with each other in her womb, so she turned to the Lord and asked why.

"And the Lord answered her, 'Two nations are in your womb, two separate peoples shall issue from your body; one people shall be mightier than the other, and the older shall serve the younger'" (Gen. 25:23). That prophecy was quite unusual, since the firstborn son usually received the father's inheritance and blessing. They called the firstborn son Esau[1] because he had a red, hairy mantle all over his body. The twin brother emerged holding on to the first's heel, and they named him Jacob.[2]

Isaac favored Esau, while Rebekah was partial to Jacob. One event changed the direction of the boys' lives. Esau had come home hungry and saw that Jacob had a pot of lentil stew cooking. He demanded something to eat. Jacob said, "First, sell me your birthright." Esau replied, "I'm at the point of death, so what use is my birthright?" Then Jacob made Esau swear to him to give him his birthright.

This and a subsequent episode created enmity between the brothers and caused great suffering later. But their father, Isaac, continued to receive God's blessings, as had Abraham.

When a famine caused great concern to Isaac, he considered moving to Egypt where he thought he could feed his family and livestock. But God came to him and told him not to go. He promised him that if he would stay and live in the land that He would point out to him, then God would be with him and bless him, just as He had promised Abraham. And if Isaac would follow His instructions, God would "fulfill the oath that I swore to your father, Abraham." The Lord would make Isaac and his descendents "as numerous as the stars of heaven" and would give them the lands they inhabited so that his succeeding generations would bless all nations.

And why did God continue to keep His promise, His covenant, to Isaac? Because "Abraham obeyed Me and kept My charge; My commandments, My laws, and My teachings" (Gen. 26:4).

Isaac did what the Lord told him and stayed in Gerar. And the Lord blessed him. He grew richer until the inhabitants became envious. Abimelech told Isaac to leave because he and his household had become too great to remain in that land. After departing, he camped in different places until he went up to Beersheba.

"That night the Lord appeared to him and said, 'I am the God of your father Abraham. Fear not, for I am with you, and I will bless you and increase your offspring for the sake of My servant Abraham. So he built an altar there and invoked the Lord by name" (verse 24).

Remember that Jacob had traded a pot of lentil stew for Esau's birthright? This same attitude of deceit occurred again when Isaac was old and his eyes were growing dim. He called Esau to him and asked him to go out and kill some game and prepare something for him to eat "so that I may give you my innermost blessing before I die" (Gen. 27:4).

Rebekah was listening, and she told Jacob to go to the flock of sheep and bring back two choice lambs. Then she would prepare a dish of food for him to take to his father so that he would receive the blessing. But Jacob knew that Isaac would recognize him because of his smooth skin. "If my father touches me, I shall appear to him as a trickster and bring upon myself a curse, not a blessing" (verse 12). Rebekah told him to do as she said, adding that the curse would be on her head instead.

Jacob did succeed in receiving the blessing, but when Esau returned and Isaac discovered he'd been deceived, Esau was enraged and totally despondent, harboring a grudge against his brother and vowing to kill Jacob once the mourning period following Isaac's death was over. To avoid this, Rebekah sent Jacob off to live with her brother Laban. Instructing him to take a wife from among Laban's daughters, she said "May El Shaddai bless you, make you fertile and numerous, so that you become an assembly of peoples. May He grant the blessing of Abraham to you and your offspring, that you may possess the land where you are sojourning, which God assigned to Abraham" (Gen. 28:3).

This doesn't sound as though Jacob had the same kind of qualities that Isaac and Abraham had, does it? Would God bless such a person? And could God's son come from such deceitful people?

When Jacob left Beersheba, he headed for Haran. As the sun had set, he stopped for the night. Using a stone for a pillow, he lay down to sleep. While Jacob was sleeping, he had a dream in which he saw a staircase or ladder beginning on earth but whose top reached into the heavens. Angels of God ascended and descended it.

Then Jacob saw God standing beside him. "I am the Lord [YHWH]," He said, "the God of your father Abraham and the God of Isaac: the ground on which you are lying I will assign to you and to your offspring. Your descendents shall be as the dust of the earth; you shall spread out to the west and to the east, to the north and to the south. All the families of the earth shall bless themselves by you and your descendants. Remember, I am with you: I will protect you wherever you go and will bring you back to this land. I will not leave you until I have done what I have promised you.

"Jacob awoke from his sleep and said, 'Surely the Lord is present in this place, and I did not know it!' Shaken, he said, 'How awesome is this place! This is none other than the abode of God, and that is the gateway to heaven.' Early in the morning, Jacob took the stone that he had put under his head and set it up as a pillar and poured oil on the top of it. He named that site Bethel; but previously the name of the city had been Luz.

"Jacob then made a vow, saying, 'If God remains with me, if He protects me on this journey that I am making, and gives me bread to eat and clothing to wear, and if I return safe to my father's house—the Lord shall be my God. And this stone, which I have set up as a pillar, shall be God's abode; and of all that You give me, I will set aside a tithe for You'" (verses 10-21).

The patriarch had a lot to learn yet, for his experiences afterward tested his patience, but he remained faithful to God, calling on His name during his many trials. Twenty years passed. Although he had increased in goods and flocks, he was still in exile and yearned to return to his homeland. But he feared the reception he would get from his twin brother, Esau, whom he had cheated out of his birthright by deceiving their father.

But Jacob decided to return home anyway, sending gifts ahead to smooth his homecoming. As extra protection he had his entire household—wives, servants, and 11 children—cross the river, while he remained behind alone. Scripture says that "a man wrestled with him until the break of dawn. When he saw that he had not prevailed against him, he wrenched Jacob's hip at its socket, so that the socket of his hip was strained as he wrestled with him. Then he said, 'Let me go, for dawn is breaking.' But he [Jacob] answered, 'I will not let you go, unless you bless me.' Said the other, 'What is your name?' He replied, 'Jacob.' Said he, 'Your name shall no longer be Jacob, but Israel, for you have striven with beings[3] divine and human, and have prevailed.' Jacob asked, 'Pray tell me your name.' But he said, 'You must not ask my name!' And he took leave of him there. So Jacob named the place Peniel,[4] meaning, 'I have seen a divine being face to face, yet my life has been preserved'" (Gen. 32:23-31).

Did Jacob wrestle with an angel or God Himself? It says "a man," but Jacob was convinced it was a divine being. Who could it have been? In Genesis who has the authority to name or to change names? I believe the being was God in the form of a man and not an angel.

Let's look at Genesis 35:1-5 where God tells Jacob to go to Bethel and build an altar to the God that appeared when he was running away from his brother. The Bible first mentions Bethel as one of the places where his grandfather Abraham built an altar and invoked the name of the Lord (see Gen. 12:6-9).

So Jacob did as God asked. He told his household to get rid of all their idols, to purify themselves, and change their clothes. This may have meant taking a ritual bath. It is symbolic to me of making a new start—just as the changing of the name from Jacob to Israel does.

Everyone did as Jacob asked. They took all their idols and their pierced earrings out of their ears and buried them. Then he said they were going up to Bethel to build an altar "to the God who answered me when I was in distress and who has been with me wherever I have gone."

And because Isaac kept his covenant with God, God protected him and his household. He caused a terror to fall upon the cities around his encampment "so that they did not pursue the sons of Jacob."

When Jacob arrived in Bethel, God met him there and blessed him. He repeated what the "being" had said to him when Jacob wrestled with him at Peniel, formally changing Jacob's name to Israel. Do you remember in that passage that Jacob had begged the person at the time to tell him His name and He refused? This time, God says to Jacob, "I am El Shaddai." And in this personage, He repeats the covenant He has made with his father, Isaac, and grandfather, Abraham. If Israel follows in His ways, God will bless him with children and grandchildren. Kings will come from his lineage and the lands will belong to his descendants.

So Jacob did as he was told. He set up a pillar on the site, poured oil on it, and called it Bethel.

Here again is the God of Abraham, Isaac, and Jacob (the latter now called Israel), from whose lineage all of humanity will be blessed. "Kings shall issue from your loins."

So where have all these prophecies taken us? In our search in Scripture for the Son of God or references to the Messiah, we have seen verses pertaining to heavenly beings and that the Hebrew *Elohim* speaks of God in the plural form. We have discovered that the all-knowing, omniscient God is to be called YHWH. In the book of Exodus, God told Moses to say to Pharaoh that Israel was His firstborn son. Was it meant simply in the spiritual sense, or will there be other sons of God—perhaps daughters as well? If so, where does Scripture refer to them? And how does God's firstborn son, Israel, figure into this mystery? I believe the Scriptures make it perfectly clear that in both the spiritual as well as physical sense, God's special blessing for humanity was to come through the genealogy of the first Hebrew (Abraham) right down the line.

The God of Abraham, Isaac, and Jacob is the same, though He was called by many names and came to them both as spirit and in the form of a man. He kept His word — His covenant, His promise, His bargain — with His people, His firstborn son, Israel, throughout the generations. The Lord continued to bless those who upheld the covenant with Him.

This same blessing was passed down to Jacob's son Joseph, sold into slavery as a young boy by his jealous brothers. But *Joseph was faithful to the God of his fathers*, and God blessed and sustained him in Egypt, raising him to a high station in Pharaoh's service. Joseph's life there and how he repaid his brothers with kindness and many material goods is living proof of the type of person God promised the world would be blessed by.

When Jacob (Israel) was old, he summoned his son Joseph. Joseph brought along his two sons, Manasseh and Ephraim, who had been born to him while he was in Egypt. Jacob told the story to Joseph of how El Shaddai had appeared to him at Lux in the land of Canaan and promised him that he would be blessed with many children and that the land in which they were living (Canaan) would someday belong to his children and their descendants to all generations. Then he told Joseph that Ephraim and Manasseh would be counted among Jacob's own sons.

The reason he did this was because his beloved wife, Rachel, had died following the birth of their son Benjamin. Jacob loved Rachel intensely and shared her heartache of having been barren for so many years. I believe this "adopting" his grandsons as his own illustrates that depth of feeling he had for Rachel.

Crossing his arms and placing his hands upon the boys' heads—his right hand on the younger son's head—Jacob asked that "in them may my name be recalled and the names of my fathers Abraham and Isaac, and may they be teeming multitudes upon the earth."

Jacob's 12 sons could spawn many multitudes. But from which one would the Messiah, the Son of God, come?

The prophecy that reveals this begins in Genesis 49 where Jacob calls his sons together. "O sons of Jacob," he says, "listen to your father, Israel." The significance of his name here shows both the physical and spiritual person. Jacob produced 12 sons while Israel symbolizes the one whom God has called to lead.

I really enjoy reading the passage because it shows me as a parent not only how much Jacob loved his children, but how well he knew their characters. God knows us as Jacob knew his children—our strengths and our weaknesses, our good points and bad. (Compare the nuances of the words used in both the Tanakh and the NKJV. The terminologies are different, but enlightening as they translate the Hebrew into English.)

As he describes each son and what fate will befall him, he tells Judah something extremely important. It is one of those milestones, markers, guideposts in our search for the Messiah.

He says, "The scepter shall not depart from Judah, nor the ruler's staff from between his feet; so that tribute shall come to him and the homage of peoples be his" (Gen. 49:10). The footnote in the Tanakh on the word "him" reads "Shiloh, 'tribute to him,' following Midrash; cf. Isa. 18:7. Meaning of Hebrew uncertain; lit. "Until he comes to Shiloh."

Speaking of the name Shiloh, the Midrash Rabbah on Lamentations, chapter 1, section 51, says: "The school of R. Shila said: The Messiah's name is 'Shiloh,' as it is stated, Until Shiloh come (Gen. 49:10)."

The prophet Isaiah is considered to be one of the greatest of the Hebrew prophets. He prophesied between 740 and 701 B.C.E., and his message stressed the holiness of God and the urgency of having faith in Him. His concern was for all people as he spoke against the evils of the time — injustice to the poor and the defiling of the sacrifice through unethical conduct.

Isaiah stressed the need for the Israelites to have faith in God rather than through alliances with other nations. The vision he received from God prophesied of the time "at the end of days" when God would establish peace throughout all the earth. It was Isaiah who foretold that a scion of David would rule with wisdom and justice, and that all the nations would flock to Jerusalem, from which would come forth the word of the Lord.

Early in the book of Isaiah the Lord spoke to Ahaz, the son of Jotham, the son of Uzziah, king of Judah, saying: "Ask for a sign from the Lord your God, anywhere down to Sheol or up to the sky" (Isa. 7:11). But Ahaz refused to do so. "Therefore the Lord himself will give you a sign: The virgin will be with child and will give birth to a son, and will call him Immanuel [the Lord With Us]. He will eat curds and honey when he knows enough to reject the wrong and choose the right. But before the boy knows enough to reject the wrong and choose the right, the land of the two kings you dread will be laid waste" (verses 14-16, NIV).

Again in Isaiah 9:6 he prophesies: "For a child has been

born to us, a son has been given us. And authority has settled on his shoulders. He has been named 'the Mighty God is planning grace; the Eternal Father, a peaceable ruler'—in token of abundant authority and of peace without limit upon David's throne and kingdom, that it may be firmly established in justice and equity now and evermore. The zeal of the Lord of Hosts shall bring this to pass."

So now we are told that among the people of Israel, the firstborn son of God, a child would be born to a virgin. We know what He will be called and what His mission will be— "The government will be upon His shoulder. And *His name will be called Wonderful, Counselor, Mighty God, Everlasting Father, Prince of Peace*" (verse 6, NKJV). And what is most exciting— what gives us the most hope and promise—is the dream of all generations that there will be no end to the peace His reign will bring.

How will we know for certain who this Child, this Son of the people of Israel, this Son of God, will be? What will be the signs?

Isaiah 11:1, 2 tells from what genealogical line this Child will come (and here is where the begats come in and point us toward the Messiah):

"There shall come forth a Rod from the stem of Jesse, and a Branch shall grow out of his roots. The Spirit of the Lord shall rest upon Him, the Spirit of wisdom and understanding, the Spirit of counsel and might, the Spirit of knowledge and of the fear of the Lord" (NKJV).

"And shall make him of quick understanding in the fear of the Lord: and he shall not judge after the sight of his eyes, neither reprove after the hearing of his ears:

"But with righteousness shall he judge the poor, and reprove with equity for the meek of the earth: and he shall smite the earth with the rod of his mouth, and with the breath of his lips shall he slay the wicked.

"And righteousness shall be the girdle of his loins, and faithfulness the girdle of his reins.

"The wolf also shall dwell with the lamb, and the leopard shall lie down with the kid; and the calf and the young lion and the fatling together; and a little child shall lead them.

"And the cow and the bear shall feed; their young ones shall lie down together: and the lion shall eat straw like the ox. And the sucking child shall play on the hole of the asp, and the weaned child shall put his hand on the cockatrice' den. They shall not hurt nor destroy in all my holy mountain: for the earth shall be full of the knowledge of the Lord, as the waters cover the sea" (verses 3-6, KJV).

The Targum (Jewish paraphrase and commentary) to Isaiah reads: "His name is called from of old, Wonderful Counsellor, Mighty God. He who lives forever, the Anointed One (or, Messiah)."

Zechariah 6:12 says: "Behold, a man called the Branch shall branch out from the place where he is, and he shall build the Temple of the Lord. He shall build the Temple of the Lord and shall assume majesty, and he shall sit on his throne and rule." Zechariah 3:8 also refers to "My servant the Branch," which he says will be a sign to them. (A footnote in the Tanakh version says that these references mean "the future king of David's line.") Some English versions render the Hebrew noun *tsemach* in these passages as "branch" or "sprout."

Jeremiah 23:5 reads: "See, a time is coming—declares the Lord—when I will raise up a true branch of David's line. He shall reign as king and shall prosper, and he shall do what is just and right in the land. In his days Judah shall be delivered and Israel shall dwell secure." The passage also uses the Hebrew word *tsemach*. The Targum to Jeremiah interprets this passage as "I will raise up for David the Messiah the Just."

The Talmudic sages, in their comment on Jeremiah 23:5, said: "This refers to the Messiah, of whom it also states, I will raise unto David a righteous shoot."

"And this is his name whereby he shall be called, THE LORD [YHWH] OUR RIGHTEOUSNESS" (Jer. 23:6, KJV; also translated as "vindicator"). The Talmud recognized the passage as referring to the Messiah.

Psalm 2:7 says: "Let me tell of the decree: the Lord said to me, 'You are My son, I have fathered you this day.'" Then in 2 Samuel 7:13, 14 the Lord declares that His servant David will build a house for "My name, and I will establish his royal throne forever. I will be a father to him, and he shall be a son to Me."

Psalm 89:4 quotes God as announcing: "I have made a covenant with My chosen one; I have sworn to My servant David: I will establish your offspring forever, I will confirm your throne for all generations." The psalmist refers to David as "my servant" and then in verses 27-29 tells that "he will say to Me, 'You are my father, my God, the rock of my deliverance.' I will appoint him first-born, highest of the kings of the earth. I will maintain My steadfast love for him always; my covenant with him shall endure." And later in verses 35-37, the Lord says: "I will not violate My covenant, or change what I have uttered. I have sworn by My holiness, once and for all; I will not be false to David. His line shall continue forever, his throne, as the sun before Me, as the moon, established forever, an enduring witness in the sky."

So what we see here is a prophecy that a child will be born to the people of Israel, who will embody the righteousness of the Lord God (YHWH), and He would come from the genealogical line of Abraham, Isaac, Jacob, and David. And again we see the term firstborn in a father-son relationship.

That prophecy has led countless Hebrew young women and men to believe that their own son might be the Messiah that Isaiah foretold. At the birth of each child they wondered, "Could this be the Holy One?" David had many descendants. When Solomon was anointed, many must have thought he might be the Messiah. After all, he fulfilled the prophecy of building a house of the Lord (the holy Temple in Jerusalem) that became the cultural and religious center of the nation. People also regarded him as a man of great wisdom and judgment. But was he the Messiah, the Son of God whom Israel awaited?

There were and continue to be those who declare themselves to be the Messiah. Some believe that each generation produces its own Messiah. I can remember reading in the Passover Haggadah a passage that declares that in each generation evil men plot against Israel, but God raises up someone to lead it out of difficulty.

So if this is true, how shall we know who the true Messiah is? If the Bible speaks of David as God's son and both Israel and David as God's firstborn, how can we know for certain who the Messiah is? Fortunately God does not leave us to just wonder. The Scriptures have provided still more guideposts. Prophecy throughout the ages gives us guidelines.

Isaiah points us to "the law and to the testimony! If they do not speak according to this word, it is because there is no light in them" (Isa. 8:20, NKJV). That is where we must go—to the Holy Scriptures. For they cast light on our feet as we walk in search of the Messiah. Did you notice the way I worded that? I did not say the search for *a* Messiah, because, as we have just seen, there have been many claimants. Like you, I want to know what God has in store for us. And it is only by asking His divine guidance that we will discover His plan.

---

[1] Synonym of *seir*, a play on the Hebrew *se'ar*, "hair."
[2] Play on Hebrew *'aqeb*, "heel."
[3] Or "God [Elohim connected with the second part of 'Israel'] and men."
[4] Understood as the "face of God."

6

The Unity
of God

Shema Yisroel, Adonai Eloheinu, Adonai Echad—
Hear, O Israel, the Lord Our God, the Lord Is One

Ever since I was a small child, I had looked up over the door of the old *shul* next to our synagogue and read these words in Hebrew and English. Somehow I felt smug and proud to be part of God's chosen people. There was something special about us and the fact that our God was the only one in the universe. We had an inner knowledge that everyone else was worshiping an inferior or fake deity. Though my friends who worshiped Jesus—Christians—also felt their God was the true and only God, I could never understand how a human being could be of flesh but at the same time divine. God *and* man? And too, what was the Trinity they spoke of? If God is one, then how could He be two or even three?

Let's look at the Holy Scriptures for some light. As we shall see, the plurality of God is a Hebrew phenomenon, not something made up by followers of Christ. It is truly a Jewish concept.

King David, God's beloved, the sweet singer of Israel and writer of psalms, recognized the complexity of God when he wrote:

"The Lord [YHWH] said to my lord ['Adoni], 'Sit at My right hand while I make your enemies your footstool.' The Lord will stretch forth from Zion your mighty scepter; hold sway over your enemies! Your people come forward willingly on your day of battle. In majestic holiness, from the womb, from the dawn, yours was the dew of youth. The Lord has sworn and will not relent, 'You are a priest forever, a rightful king by My decree [or after the manner of Melchizedek].' The Lord ['Adoni] is at your right hand" (Ps. 110:1-5).

The psalm mentions two divine beings: the Lord (YHWH) and the lord ('Adonai). Usually the word "Lord" appears as the plural form 'Adonai in the Hebrew, but when "my" is used with it, it takes the singular possessive form 'Adoni.

Now notice that the first line in the English translation reads: "The Lord said to my lord." This may not be easy to understand, but observe in many modern translations that the first "Lord" is spelled with a large capital and three small capital letters, while the second "Lord" has only the first letter capitalized and the rest in lowercase letters. What does that mean?

Whenever you see in the English Bible the word "Lord" in one large and three small capital letters, the corresponding term in the Hebrew text is the tetragrammaton (YHWH). But the English word "Lord" with only one capital and three lowercase letters corresponds to 'Adonai in the Hebrew text.

Thus, the English rendering of the Hebrew in Psalm 110:1 is "The Lord [YHWH] saith unto my Lord ['Adonai]."

The Hebrew shows that the passage refers to two distinct persons, each bearing a divine name. But to whom is the Lord speaking? He is speaking to none other than the Messiah, called in this text "my Lord ['Adoni]."

This Bible passage indicates that the Godhead is what we may properly term a uniplural or compound unity, but not a sole or absolute unity. It is an *'echad* (unity), as stated in Deuteronomy 6:4: "The Lord our God, the Lord is one!" (NKJV). But not a *yachid* (sole unity), as the latter Hebrew term denotes. Notice that in the first verse the Lord says to the psalmist's Lord ('Adoni), the Messiah: "Sit on My right hand," that is, in the position of authority, power, and honor next to that of the Lord Himself.

Let us now consider Proverbs 8:12-36. Notice that the term "wisdom" is personified. Verse 12 begins: "I, Wisdom." In this case, it is represented in *'echad* relationship to the Lord. We are speaking of a person here. Surely, then, this refers to the Messiah.

What do we read in this text? In verses 22 and 23 the speaker says: "The Lord created me at the beginning of His course as the first of His works of old. In the distant past I was fashioned, at the beginning, at the origin of earth."

Take notice of verses 24 to 36: "There was still no deep when I was brought forth, no springs rich in water; before [the foundation of] the mountains were sunk, before the hills I was born. He [Yahweh] had not yet made earth and fields, or the world's first clumps of clay. I was there when He set the heavens into place; when He fixed the horizon upon the deep; when He made the heavens above firm, and the fountains of the deep gushed forth; when He assigned the sea its limits, so that its waters never transgress His command; when He fixed the foundations of the earth, I was with Him as a confidant, a source of delight every day, rejoicing before Him at all times, rejoicing in His inhabited world, finding delight with mankind. Now, sons, listen to me; happy are they who keep my ways. Heed discipline and become wise; do not spurn it. Happy is the man who listens to me, coming early to my gates each day, waiting outside my doors. For he who finds me finds life and obtains favor from the Lord [YAHWEH]. But he who misses me destroys himself; all who hate me love death." (See the NKJV for different language.)

This language is very clear. Here we see that YHWH had someone else with Him before the creation of the world. To whom was God speaking? Not angels, but God's Son, the Messiah.

The ancient Jewish teachers, in the talmudic writings, recognized the preexistence of the Messiah. Commenting on Psalm 72:17, the Talmud states:

"The name of the Messiah, as it is written, *His* [sc. the Messiah's] *name shall endure for ever, and has existed before the sun!*—I will tell you: only its [the sun's] cavity was created before the world was created, but its fire [was created] on the eve of the Sabbath"—Pesachim 54a, Babylonian Talmud.

We have already read in Proverbs that the Messiah was with God during Creation. Now let us turn to Genesis 1:26, 27: "And God said, 'Let us make man in our image, after our likeness. . . . And God created man in His image, in the image of God He created him; male and female He created them."

To whom was God speaking when He said, "Let us"? According to the Holy Scriptures, as we just saw explained in

Proverbs, He was talking to the Prince of the universe, God's Son, the Messiah.

Let's talk about angels for a moment. Some religious groups claim that Jesus was an angel on the same level as Lucifer, who is called Satan. Was He? Let's look and see what the Bible tells us about the nature of God's Son and the role of angels. The root of the Hebrew word for angels means "to send." Heavenly beings, they act as intermediaries—messengers between God and man. Their role in heaven is to be servants to God and to worship Him. That is not the role of God or the Son of God.

Hebrews 1 refutes the idea that Jesus was only another angel. It explains that God had spoken directly to the patriarchs and through the prophets. But more recently He had communicated to people through His Son.

Verses 4, 5, and 6 show that Jesus is higher than the angels because "He has by inheritance obtained a more excellent name than they." To which of the angels had God ever said, "You are My Son, Today I have begotten You?" (quoting Psalm 2:7).

Psalm 97:7 declares that "all divine beings bow down to Him." Their function is to be ministering spirits to those who will inherit salvation (see Heb. 1:7, 14; Ps. 104:4).

King David asked the question about the relationship between God, humanity, and the angels in Psalm 8. "What is man that You are mindful of him, mortal man that You have taken note of him, that You have made him little less than divine (or the angels)." So we see here in this passage that man is lower than the angels God created to minister to Him and human beings. In Genesis God had given Adam dominion (to be ruler, lord, and master) over all that He had created. But

He did not call Adam His Son. Scripture differentiates between man and angels; angels and God; God the Father and God the Son. As far as we know God did not create angels from the dust of the earth. They are spirit and in the spirit realm. Was God's spiritual and earthly son an angel? I am certain He was not.

We really need to look at the Hebrew references in the first verse of the first chapter of Genesis that use words indicating more than one person in the Godhead: "In the beginning God ['Elohim] created the heaven and the earth" (verse 1). The Hebrew word 'Elohim literally means "Gods." The singular form is 'Eloah ("God"). Therefore, the verse could read: "In the beginning Gods [or the Godhead] created the heaven and the earth." The word "God" appears more than 30 times in the first chapter of Genesis, and in Hebrew it is in the plural form 'Elohim.

Describing what God created on the sixth day, verse 26 says: "And God ['Elohim] said: Let us make man in our image, after our likeness." The plural pronoun "us" also appears in Genesis 3:22 where it says: "And the Lord [YHWH] God ['Elohim] said, 'Behold, the man is become as one of us, to know good and evil.'"

And the Creation story is not the only place to refer to God in the plural form. In Genesis 11:6, 7, when God [YHWH] saw that Noah's descendants planned to build a tower in order to make a name for themselves, Scripture records that God said, "Let us go down and there confound their language.'"

Again we ask, Whom was the Lord addressing when He said, "Let us"?

Rashi, the noted Jewish commentator, suggests that God

was addressing angels. Angels, however, are themselves created beings. Therefore, they cannot create. Furthermore, the Scripture declares that man was created "in the image of God." Nowhere does Holy Writ state that human beings were created in the image of the angels.

It was evidently another divine Being whom God addressed when He said, "Let us make man." But who was that other divine Being? Again, He was none other than the Son of God, the Messiah.

There is only one God the Father, who rules the universe. But seated with Him on His throne is His Associate, whom He calls His Anointed One, or Messiah. This second Person is a member of the royal household of the universe. Therefore, the word "God" is a generic term used to denote a deity or divine being, and as such it can apply to both the Father and to His anointed Son, the Messiah.

But what about the *Shema* (the traditional Jewish name for Deuteronomy 6:4)? Isn't it translated at times "Hear, O Israel, the Lord our God is one Lord"? Yes, but that isn't the way it reads in the Hebrew. To begin with, the word "Lord" is not at the end in that text.

In the *Shema* we should note that in Hebrew the words "our God" are in reality "our Gods" (*'Eloheinu*); thus the plural and not the singular. Hence, the more correct rendering of this very important text would be "Hear, O Israel, the Lord our Gods [*'Elohim*] is one [*'echad*]."

The Hebrew *'echad* denotes unity of a uniplural or a combined association of more than one member or party rather than a unity consisting of solely one individual member. Thus, for example, when God gave to Adam his wife, Eve, it was said of them that they became "one [*'echad*] flesh" (Gen. 2:24).

The passage declares the two parties—man and woman—to be one ['echad], a unity.

As God made the first day of the week, the record says that it consisted of two parts—evening and morning. Yet the Scripture says in Genesis 1:5 (literally): "And there was evening and there was morning; day one ['echad]." That is, the first day was a unit consisting of two parts. Ezra 2:64 literally says of all the people assembled, "All the congregation [was] as on [ki-'echad] forty-two thousand three hundred [and] sixty."

When the Bible speaks of a unit consisting of only one individual to the exclusion of every other, it uses yachid. Take for instance, the case of Abraham when God bade him to offer up his only son, Isaac: "Take now thy son, thine only [yachid] son" (Gen. 22:2).

The Hebrew word employs yachid here and not 'echad to designate a sole individual. The Shema does not say "Hear, O Israel: The Lord our God is one [yachid] Lord" as if the Deity consists of solely one divine person. Rather, it declares: "The Lord our God is one ['echad] Lord," as a uniplural, or combined membership, of divine persons.

So who is God? Is He Yahweh, our heavenly Father, or Y'shua, Jesus the Christ? And what about the Holy Spirit? Could They be one and the same—the names used interchangeably—or three separate persons? I have always found it confusing to know to whom I should pray.

As a mother and homemaker, while making challah bread for Sabbath, I looked at the ingredients on my table—flour, yeast, oil, eggs, water, and salt. Before I combined them, they were separate entities. But once mixed together, they assumed a new form. They became dough. And from that one combined stuff I was able to make many things—challah (the braided bread), rolls, and many shapes called by other names. But in essence, the final product came from the dough. I was able to see a corollary in this simple domestic process with the Godhead.

God the Father, Jesus the Son, and the Holy Spirit are all separate persons with different purposes, different reasons for being. Yet they are one. Now I understand why my Catholic friends pray, "In the name of the Father, the Son, and the Holy Spirit." For They are all God and for us fulfill specific purposes.

Even the disciples were confused on this subject because it is a difficult concept. Despite having shared the life of Y'shua (the form of Jesus' name in New Testament times) for three years, they still did not understand His Messiahship until He had been resurrected from the dead following His crucifixion by the Romans.

Matthew 28 makes this evident. Remember, each of the disciples was waiting for Jesus to set up a kingdom on this earth in which they would be chief players. Despite the fact that He Himself told them that His kingdom was not of this earth, they were still unable to completely understand that concept.

"And when they saw Him, they worshiped Him; but some doubted. Then Jesus came and spoke to them, saying, 'All authority has been given to Me in heaven and on earth. Go therefore and make disciples of all the nations, baptizing them in the name of the Father and of the Son and of the Holy Spirit, teaching them to observe all things that I have commanded you; and lo, I am with you always, even to the end of the age'" (verses 17-20, NKJV).

Such language outraged the Jewish leaders of Jesus' time. They realized that He was equating Himself with

YHWH, putting Himself on an equal plane with God, even speaking of Himself in that way in the same breath. It was blasphemy—sacrilege! Even today if you should suggest to a rabbi or a Jew that Jesus is part of the Godhead, you'd be challenged and ostracized.

Even my own father, raised in an Orthodox Jewish home, with the traditional Jewish education, denied Y'shua. Once I returned from college for the weekend carrying a suitcase of religious books for a course I was taking in comparative theology at Boston University. When he saw books on Christ in the bag, he opened the front door of our house and literally threw them out into the street. My mother, whom he loved and adored, is Irish and was raised a Christian. All that affection he felt for her obviously was not strong enough for him to get above his gut-level reaction. Christ, to him, was the reason the Jews have suffered persecution from all the nations on earth, and my father was not about to have any books written about Jesus in our house. The Holocaust of Nazi Germany was fresh in his mind, and though it had affected none of our immediate family so far as I know, we did have Jews who had been liberated from concentration camps in our community. I remember hearing their hushed voices, their words of anguish; I remember seeing the tears and pain reflected in their eyes, the numbers tattooed into their skin. As an adult now, having greater knowledge of what Jews (including my father) feared at the time, I understand his reaction.

The apostle Paul writes about a similar hostility in 2 Corinthians 3:12-18. There he explains why he speaks with boldness about Christ, "unlike Moses, who put a veil over his face so that the children of Israel could not look steadily at the end of what was passing away. But their minds were hardened. For until this day the same veil remains unlifted in the reading of the Old Testament, because the veil is taken away in Christ. But even to this day, when Moses is read, a veil lies on their heart. Nevertheless when one turns to the Lord, the veil is taken away.

"Now the Lord is the Spirit; and where the Spirit of the Lord is, there is liberty. But we all, with unveiled face, beholding as in a mirror the glory of the Lord, are being transformed into the same image from glory to glory, just as by the Spirit of the Lord" (NKJV).

The New Testament reveals to us Christ's existence, purpose, and ministry. It is also where we find what has come to be known as the Trinity. Writing to the church at Corinth, the apostle Paul says: "Therefore concerning the eating of things offered to idols, we know that an idol is nothing in the world, and that there is no other God but one. For even if there are so-called gods, whether in heaven or on earth (as there are many gods and many lords), yet for us there is only one God, the Father, of whom are all things, and we for Him; and one Lord Jesus Christ, through whom are all things, and through whom we live" (1 Cor. 8:4-6, NKJV).

In 1 Corinthians 2:7-16 Paul explains the Holy Spirit: "But we speak the wisdom of God in a mystery, the hidden wisdom which God ordained before the ages for our glory, which none of the rulers of this age knew; for had they known, they would not have crucified the Lord of glory. But as it is written: 'Eye has not seen, nor ear heard, nor have entered into the heart of man the things which God has prepared for those who love Him.'

"But God has revealed them to us through His Spirit. For the Spirit searches all things, yes, the deep things of God. For what man knows the things of a man except the spirit of the man which is in him? Even so no one knows the things of God except the Spirit of God.

"Now we have received, not the spirit of the world, but the Spirit who is from God, that we might know the things that have been freely given to us by God. These things we also speak, not in words which man's wisdom teaches but which the Holy Spirit teaches, comparing spiritual things with spiritual.

"But the natural man does not receive the things of the Spirit of God, for they are foolishness to him; nor can he know them, because they are spiritually discerned. But he who is spiritual judges all things, yet he himself is rightly judged by no one. For 'Who has known the mind of the Lord that he may instruct Him?' But we have the mind of Christ" (NKJV).

So Paul, through the Holy Spirit, was able to discern the importance and place of each member of the Godhead and gives us instruction as to the purpose of the Holy Spirit—revealing the mind of God through Christ.

Writing to the Ephesians, Paul explains "that the God of our Lord Jesus Christ, the Father of glory, may give to you the spirit of wisdom and revelation in the knowledge of Him" (Eph. 1:17, NKJV).

And to the churches of Galatia, he added: "The fruit of the Spirit is love, joy, peace, longsuffering, kindness, goodness, faithfulness, gentleness, self control" (Gal. 5:22, 23, NKJV).

This shows Paul's understanding of the intertwining, the unity, of YHWH, Christ, and the Holy Spirit—each working together for the salvation of humanity.

7

The Messiah in Prophecy

Throughout this book I have been using the term *Messiah*. But what does it mean? The word comes from the Hebrew *Mashiach*, "an anointed one." The term appears 39 times in the Old Testament and hundreds of times in the New Testament. *Anoint* in the biblical sense means "to smear or pour oil or other unctuous substance upon." The Jews recognized at least three uses of anointing: (1) ordinary anointing for the purpose of personal hygiene; (2) official anointing, which prophets, priests, and kings received at or before their accession to office; (3) anointing as an adjunct to healing—sometimes in a medicinal sense.

The Hebrew Scriptures refer to the kings of Israel as the "anointed of the Lord." But here we are looking at the use of the term *Mashiach* as it relates to the expected king and deliverer of God's people, Israel.

Throughout their history the Jewish people have looked forward to the coming of the Messiah—the Anointed—as foretold by the prophets in Scripture. They waited expectantly for the Holy One who would be the embodiment of priest, prophet, and king, and who would be descended from the line of David. The Holy Scriptures contain abundant clues and references to this deliverer and redeemer of Israel.

For example, Jeremiah 23:5, 6 announces: "See, a time is coming—declares the Lord—when I will raise up a true branch of David's line. He shall reign as king and shall prosper, and he shall do what is just and right in the land. In his days Judah shall be delivered and Israel shall dwell secure. And this is the name by which he shall be called: 'The Lord is our Vindicator [also translated righteousness].'"

Isaiah 11:1-10 also speaks of the Messiah's heritage coming as a "shoot out of the stump of Jesse." But the passage tells us much more than just genealogy. It details His character and is a major guidepost in our search for the Messiah. Filled with the Holy Spirit the Messiah will judge us not through His senses or through His mortal understanding. This passage has great significance for us as a criteria in judging any individual who claims to be the Messiah. In addition, it tells us what His kingdom will consist of. This passage in Isaiah gives me and, I hope, you the hope of living forever with God in a land of peace.

"But a shoot shall grow out of the stump of Jesse,
A twig shall sprout from his stock.
The spirit of the Lord shall alight upon him:
A spirit of wisdom and insight,
A spirit of counsel and valor,
A spirit of devotion and reverence for the Lord.

He shall sense the truth by his reverence for the Lord:
He shall not judge by what his eyes behold,
Nor decide by what his ears perceive.
Thus he shall judge the poor with equity
And decide with justice for the lowly of the land.
He shall strike down a land with the rod of his mouth
And slay the wicked with the breath of his lips.
Justice shall be the girdle of his loins,
And faithfulness the girdle of his waist.
The wolf shall dwell with the lamb,
The leopard lie down with the kid;
The calf, the beast of prey, and the fatling together,
With a little boy to herd them.
The cow and the bear shall graze,
Their young shall lie down together;
And the lion, like the ox, shall eat straw.
A babe shall play
Over a viper's hole,
And an infant pass his hand
Over an adder's den.
In all of My sacred mount
Nothing evil or vile shall be done;
For the land shall be filled with devotion to the Lord
As water covers the sea.
In that day,
The stock of Jesse that has remained standing
Shall become a standard to peoples —
Nations shall seek his counsel
And his abode shall be honored."

The prophet reveals not only the Messiah's genealogical background but also what kind of person He will be — His character. Though He is human, He will possess the spirit of the Lord. And because of His reverence for God, the kingdom He establishes will be one of peace and safety—even for little children playing among the fiercest beasts. And He will be the one to whom all will come and seek wisdom.

In the book of Numbers the prophet Balaam tells that the time of His coming "is not yet, what I behold will not be soon: a star rises from Jacob, a scepter comes forth from Israel" (Num. 24:17). It's those begats again. We need to go back and find out in whose line this Messiah will appear.

That means way back to God's promise to Abraham in Genesis 17, where God tells him that He will make Abraham the father of a multitude of nations and will maintain His covenant between Abraham and his offspring forever.

God repeats that promise to Abraham's descendants— Jacob's grandsons: "You, O Judah, your brothers shall praise. . . . The scepter shall not depart from Judah, nor the ruler's staff from between his feet; so that tribute shall come to him[1] and the homage of peoples be his" (Gen. 49:8-10).

This person would be God Himself in human form, as we read in Micah 1:2, 3: "Listen, all you peoples, give heed, O earth, and all it holds; and let my Lord God be your accuser— My Lord from His Holy abode. For Lo! the Lord is coming forth from His dwelling-place. He will come down and stride upon the heights of the earth."

Elsewhere the book of Micah provided glimpses of the Messiah's birth and birthplace. "And you, O Bethlehem of Ephrath, least among the clans of Judah, from you one shall come forth to rule Israel for Me—one whose origin is from old, from ancient times. . . . He shall stand and shepherd by the might of the Lord, by the power of the name of the Lord his God" (Micah 5:1-3).

Not only would He descend from the lineage of King David, but He would also be a prophet. "The Lord your God will raise up for you a prophet from among your own people, like myself; him you shall heed. . . . 'I will raise up a prophet for them from among their own people, like yourself: I will put My words in his mouth and he will speak to them all that I command him'" (Deut. 18:15-18).

Scripture also revealed the purpose of His coming. Earlier we looked at Isaiah 7 and 9. In Isaiah 40:5 the prophet declares that "the Presence of the Lord shall appear, and all flesh, as one, shall behold — for the Lord Himself has spoken." Malachi 3:1, 2 tells the people of Israel: "Behold, I am sending My messenger to clear the way before Me, and the Lord whom you seek shall come to His Temple suddenly. As for the angel of the covenant that you desire, he is already coming. But who can endure the day of his coming, and who can hold out when he appears?"

Isaiah 42:1-4 describes the Messiah as "My servant, whom I uphold, My chosen one, in whom I delight. I have put My spirit upon him, he shall teach the true way to the nations. He shall not cry out or shout aloud, or make his voice heard in the streets. He shall not break even a bruised reed, or snuff out even a dim wick. He shall bring forth the true way. He shall not grow dim or be bruised till he has established the true way on earth; and the coastlands shall await his teaching."

"The true way." Prophetic words. Words to heed. If one will just listen to Isaiah or study the prophecies regarding the Messiah, I do not believe there would be any question as to His identity. In my search for the Messiah, as I studied and read these passages, my resolve became firm. Please read with me Isaiah 52:13-15 and the entirety of Isaiah 53 and see for yourself the true character of the person called the Messiah. And pay strict attention to the wording because you will want to remember it in the next chapter. I call your attention to these passages because during the many years I had studied with the rabbis, none of them pointed these passages out to me. Had I read them, heard them, listened to the words, I would have immediately questioned them about whom Isaiah had in mind. I believe that the passages are so strong, so self-explanatory that there can be no question of their meaning.

"Indeed, My servant shall prosper, be exalted and raised to great heights. Just as the many were appalled at him — so marred was his appearance, unlike that of man, his form, beyond human semblance — just so he shall startle many nations. Kings shall be silenced because of him, for they shall see what has not been told them, shall behold what they never have heard.

"Who can believe what we have heard? Upon whom has the arm of the Lord been revealed? For he has grown, by His favor, like a tree crown, like a *tree trunk* out of arid ground. He had no form or beauty, that we should look at him: no charm, that we should find him pleasing. He was despised, shunned by men, a man of suffering, familiar with disease. As one who hid his face from us, he was despised, we held him of no account. Yet it was our sickness that he was bearing, our suffering that he endured. We accounted him plagued, smitten and afflicted by God; but he was wounded because of our sins, crushed because of our iniquities. He bore the chastisement that made us whole, and by his bruises we were healed. We all went astray like sheep, each going his own way; and the Lord visited upon him the guilt of all of us.

"'He was maltreated, yet he was submissive, he did not open his mouth; like a sheep being led to slaughter, like a ewe, dumb before those who shear her, he did not open his mouth. By oppressive judgment he was taken away, who could describe his abode? For he was cut off from the land of the living through the sin of my people, who deserved the punishment. And his grave was set among the wicked, and with the rich, in his death—though he had done no injustice and had spoken no falsehood. But the Lord chose to crush him by disease, that, if he made himself an offering for guilt, he might see offspring and have long life, and that through him the Lord's purpose might prosper. Out of his anguish he shall see it; he shall enjoy it to the full through his devotion.

"'My righteous servant makes the many righteous, it is their punishment that he bears; assuredly, I will give him the many as his portion, he shall receive the multitude as his spoil. For he exposed himself to death and was numbered among the sinners, whereas he bore the guilt of the many and made intercession for sinners.'"

Elsewhere Isaiah proclaims: "See, the Lord has proclaimed to the end of the earth: Announce to Fair Zion, your Deliverer is coming! See, His reward is with Him, His recompense before Him. And they shall be called, 'The Holy People, the Redeemed of the Lord'" (Isa. 62:11, 12).

The Messiah would be a king, but not in the usual sense. He would not wear regal robes, nor would He be a great military leader in the sense that He would accomplish His goals by the sword. Instead, He would be the guilt offering, the sacrifice—as a lamb of God—taking upon Himself the sins of the people yet remaining sinless Himself. The true Messiah would perish so that God's purpose of making many righteous could be fulfilled.

The prophet Zechariah provided more information on the Messiah and God's purpose in sending Him: "Rejoice greatly, Fair Zion; raise a shout, Fair Jerusalem! Lo, your king is coming to you. He is victorious, triumphant, yet humble, riding on an ass, on a donkey foaled by a she-ass. He shall banish chariots from Ephraim and horses from Jerusalem; the warrior's bow shall be banished. He shall call on the nations to surrender, and his rule shall extend from sea to sea and from ocean to land's end" (Zech. 9:9, 10).

Zechariah also pointed to the Messiah's divinity: "In that day, the Lord will shield the inhabitants of Jerusalem; and the feeblest of them shall be in that day like David, and the House of David like a divine being—like an angel of the Lord—at their head" (Zech. 12:8).

The prophet Daniel had a dream in which he saw both YHWH, whom he calls "the ancient of Days," and the Messiah: "Thrones were set in place, and the Ancient of Days took His seat. His garment was like white snow, and the hair of His head was like lamb's wool. His throne was tongues of flame; its wheels were blazing fire. A river of fire streamed forth before Him; thousands upon thousands served Him; myriads upon myriads attended Him; the court sat and the books were opened. . . .

"One like a human being came with the clouds of heaven; he reached the Ancient of Days and was presented to Him. Dominion, glory, and kingship were given to him; all peoples and nations of every language must serve him. His dominion is an everlasting dominion that shall not pass away. And his kingship, one that shall not be destroyed" (Dan. 7:9-14).

When Daniel says that His kingship shall not be destroyed, I find that particularly interesting because Scripture is rife with the history of reigns and realms wherein the subjects first adored the ruler then later maligned or even assassinated him. Such is the history of humankind. It well documents the rise and fall of empires.

But Daniel does even more than just give us a vague prophecy. He tells us when the Messiah will come by providing a definite time frame.

"Seventy weeks have been decreed for your people and your holy city until the measure of transgression is filled and that of sin complete, until iniquity is expiated, and eternal righteousness ushered in; and prophetic vision ratified [sealed], and the Holy of Holies anointed. You must know and understand: From the issuance of the word to restore and rebuild Jerusalem until the [time of the] anointed leader is seven weeks; and for sixty-two weeks it will be rebuilt, square and moat, but in a time of distress. And after those sixty-two weeks, the anointed one [Messiah] will disappear and vanish. . . . During one week he will make a firm covenant with many. For half a week he will put a stop to the sacrifice and the meal offering" (Dan. 9:24-27).

To understand this prophecy, one must make a detailed study. It has been determined that the prophetic 70 weeks equal 490 years. Beginning with the command to rebuild Jerusalem (Ezra 7:12-26) in 457 B.C.E. under Artaxerxes, king of Persia, seven weeks (49 years) went by before its actual completion in 408 B.C.E. (Ezra 6:14). From then "unto the Messiah the Prince" was a period of 62 weeks, or 434 years, which brings us to 27 C.E. Using the one-week prophecy in which the Messiah would be "cut off" in the middle of the week, we have three and a half years until the death of the Messiah (31 C.E.).

It is understandable that through the centuries many individuals were thought to be the Messiah sent by God to save His people from oppression. And throughout biblical history, were there not great leaders who appeared to be saviors? What about Abraham, the progenitor of the Jewish nation? Could he have been a type of Messiah? And Moses—surely he was the one through whom God had spoken and provided the laws by which all generations should be governed. Could he also be cut of the same cloth? How about Noah, David, and Solomon? Solomon fulfilled prophecy when he built the first Temple. Was he the Messiah?

Many individuals had performed formidable works (even miracles) that seemed to proclaim they were the long-anticipated Messiah. Even the prophets and rabbis have been confused.

From the house of David came Zerubbabel, who restored the Temple after its destruction by the Babylonians. The prophets thought he might be the Messiah. Zechariah spoke of him: "'This is the word of the Lord to Zerubbabel: Not by might, nor by power, but by My spirit—said the Lord of Hosts. Whoever you are, O great mountain in the path of Zerubbabel, turn into level ground! For he shall produce that excellent stone; it shall be greeted with shout of "Beautiful! Beautiful!"'

"And the word of the Lord came to me: 'Zerubbabel's hands have founded this House and Zerubbabel's hands shall complete it. Then you shall know it was the Lord of Hosts who sent me to you'" (Zech. 4:6-9).

But the miracles foretold in Isaiah 35 did not occur as prophesied, so the Jews continued to anticipate the true Son of God. They clung to the divine promise: "'He Himself is coming to give you triumph.' Then the eyes of the blind shall be opened, and the ears of the deaf shall be unstopped. Then the lame shall leap like a deer, and the tongue of the dumb shall shout aloud" (verses 4-6).

Throughout biblical history the prophets repeatedly speak of the time ("end of days") when a king will rule over Israel and the law of the Lord will spread from Jerusalem to all the peoples of the world. And throughout the Hebrew Scriptures we find many references to the Holy One of Israel—the righteous Root of the line of David—whom God would raise up to become the redeemer, a divinely appointed individual who would bring salvation to the Jewish people.

In Malachi 3:1 the Lord speaks of a forerunner of the Messiah: "Behold, I am sending My messenger to clear the way before Me, and the Lord whom you seek shall come to His Temple suddenly. As for the angel of the covenant that you desire, he is already coming." And in verse 23, Malachi specifies that the forerunner will be the prophet Elijah (meaning, "Yah is my God"): "Lo, I will send the prophet Elijah to you before the coming of the awesome, fearful day of the Lord."

As we have already observed, many individuals even down to this day have believed they were the embodiment of the Messiah and could bring a time of peace to the land of Israel. Truly selfless reasons inspired some, while others sought power through military might to establish themselves on the throne of David. Unfortunately, they raised the hopes of many pious and sincere Jews and gained much support, only to have their dreams crushed and plunged into despair.

One of the most famous in Jewish history to be considered the Messiah was Simeon Bar Kokhba, who led the Jewish revolt against the Romans in 131-135 C.E. His most ardent supporter was Rabbi Akiva, who referred to him as "King

Messiah." Bar Kokhba came from the town of Koziba and was known as the "Man of Koziba," but he changed his name to the "Son of the Star." Rallying a large army of Jews, he fought the Romans and even succeeded in capturing Jerusalem, defeating the Roman forces there many times. But Bar Kokhba's revolt died with him and his men, and then the Romans took revenge by killing many helpless Jewish people.[2]

Still others have become leaders of messianic movements that promised deliverance to their followers, but came only to a sad end. Approximately 10 years before the birth of Jesus, Judah the Galilean appeared. His passion for liberty led him to found a group called the Zealots. As freedom fighters they sought to establish a reign of kings who would set up a kingdom of heaven on earth to rule over God's chosen people. But the Zealots only plunged Palestine into more misery.

Theudus (44 C.E.), mentioned in the book of Acts, was beheaded by the Romans. Menachem ben Judah (d. 66 C.E.), son of Judah of Galilee, captured the palace and fortress of Masada. His successor, Eleazar ben Jair, held it for seven years, and when surrounded by the Romans, convinced his followers that it was better to die than be captured. Simeon Bar Giora acted as a Jewish military leader in the war against Rome (66-70 C.E.).

Moses of Crete (c. 440 C.E.) attempted to lead his followers through water, as did his namesake, but many drowned. Serene of Syria (c. 720 C.E.) promised release from the rule of Caliph Omar II and the authority of rabbinic Judaism. When tried for heresy, he retracted his beliefs. Abu Issa al-Isfahani founded a Jewish sect in Persia in the eighth century. A pupil of Abu's—Yehuda Yudghan—claimed to be a prophet, but his followers, the Yudghanites, believed he was the Messiah.

THE MESSIAH IN PROPHECY

Ibn Aryeh appeared in Lyons in France or Leon in Spain about 1060, and after being influenced by a dream, proclaimed himself to be the Messiah. Solomon, the Karaite Kohen of Aaronic descent, claimed: "I am the man whom Israel is waiting for." Moses Al-Dar'i became prominent in Fez, Morocco, as did David Alroy in the first half of the twelfth century in the remote eastern districts of the Muslim Empire. A Yemenite proclaimed himself Messiah in 1172, and Abraham Ben Samuel Abulafia, a Kabbalist, at the end of the thirteenth century. David Reubeni was thought to be a messiah in the sixteenth century. Shabbetai Tzevi, in the seventeenth century in Turkey, was one of the most popular messianic pretenders. His scholarship and ambitions won him many followers. When Shabbetai attempted a revolt against the sultan in Constantinople, the authorities arrested him and decreed the death penalty against him, at which point he converted to Islam. Many believed after his death that he would return as their redeemer.

Other pseudomessiahs included Berachian (1695-1740) in Turkey; Abraham Miguel Cardosa (1630-1710) in Portugal; Johnathan Eyebeschutz (1690-1764) in Poland; Jacob Frank (1726-1791) in Poland; Nathan Benjamin Halevi Ghazzati (1644-1680) in Jerusalem; Judah Chasid Halevi (1638-1700) in Podolia; Loebele Prossnitz (d. 1750) in Moravia; Jacob Querida (c. 1690) in Turkey; and Hayim Vital (Hayim Calabrese) (1543-1620) in Palestine.

Many of them started militaristic movements that planned to usher in the messianic era through might and power. But all were false messiahs. All died, and none were resurrected to live and speak with their followers. Though many appeared to fulfill some of the prophecies that foretold in detail how the

Jews would know the Messiah, only one—Jesus of Nazareth—seems to really fulfill the expectations of the prophets as written in the Holy Scriptures.

---

[1] Or "until Shiloh comes" (referring to the Messiah).
[2] *New Jewish Encyclopedia,* p. 40.

8

Jesus the Messiah

Is Jesus the Messiah long awaited by the Jews?

His disciples and first believers were Jews like Himself. Thousands of adherents from both the Gentiles and Jews believed in Him and were baptized in just one day. Though the Jewish religious establishment persecuted His disciples and followers, the Christian church continued to grow and has spread worldwide thousands of years after His death.

Let's look at those Messianic prophecies in Scripture and see if Jesus is in fact the true Messiah.

He would be born of woman—"But when the fullness of the time had come, God sent forth His Son, born of a woman, born under the law [meaning born to one who followed God's revelation as presented in the Hebrew scriptures] (Gal. 4:4, NKJV; see Gen. 3:15).

He would be descended from Abraham—"The book of

105

the genealogy of Jesus Christ, the Son of David, the Son of Abraham" (Matt. 1:1, NKJV). "And Jacob begot Joseph the husband of Mary, of whom was born Jesus who is called Christ. So all the generations from Abraham to David are fourteen generations, from David until the captivity in Babylon are fourteen generations, and from the captivity in Babylon until the Christ are fourteen generations" (verses 16, 17, NKJV).

"Now to Abraham and his Seed were the promises made. He does not say, 'And to seeds,' as of many, but as of one, 'And to your Seed,' who is Christ" (Gal. 3:16, NKJV; see Gen. 12:3; 13:15).

He would be a descendant of Isaac — "The son of Jacob, the son of Isaac, the son of Abraham, the son of Terah, the son of Nahor" (Luke 3:34, NKJV; see Gen. 17:19).

He would be a descendant of Jacob — "Abraham begot Isaac, Isaac begot Jacob, and Jacob begot Judah and his brothers" (Matt. 1:2, NKJV; see Luke 3:34; Num. 24:17, 19; Gen. 49:10).

He would come from the tribe of Judah — "The son of Amminadab, the son of Ram, the son of Hezron, the son of Perez, the son of Judah" (Luke 3:33, NKJV). "It is evident that our Lord arose from Judah, of which tribe Moses spoke nothing concerning priesthood" (Heb. 7:14, NKJV). "But one of the elders said to me, 'Do not weep. Behold, the Lion of the tribe of Judah, the Root of David, has prevailed to open the scroll and to loose its seven seals'" (Rev. 5:5, NKJV; see Ps. 78:67-71).

He would be heir to the throne of David — "He will be great, and will be called the Son of the Highest; and the Lord God will give Him the throne of His father David. And He will reign over the house of Jacob forever, and of His kingdom there will be no end" (Luke 1:32, 33, NKJV; Matt. 1:1-16; 9:27; 15:22; 21:9; see Isa. 9:5-7; 11:1-10; Ps. 132:11-18; Jer. 23:5).

He would be anointed and eternal — "But to the Son He says: 'Your throne, O God, is forever and ever; a scepter of righteousness is the scepter of Your Kingdom. You have loved righteousness and hated lawlessness; therefore God, Your God, has anointed You with the oil of gladness more than Your companions.' And: 'You, Lord, in the beginning laid the foundation of the earth, and the heavens are the work of Your hands; they will perish, but You remain; and they will all grow old like a garment; like a cloak You will fold them up, and they will be changed. But You are the same, and Your years will not fail'" (Heb. 1:8-12, NKJV; see Ps. 45:6, 7; 102:13-27).

He would be born in Bethlehem — "And Joseph also went up from Galilee, out of the city of Nazareth, into Judea, to the city of David, which is called Bethlehem, because he was of the house and lineage of David, to be registered with Mary, his betrothed wife, who was with child. . . . And she brought forth her firstborn Son, and wrapped Him in swaddling cloths, and laid Him in a manger, because there was no room for them in the inn" (Luke 2:4-7, NKJV). "Jesus was born in Bethlehem of Judea in the days of Herod the king" (Matt. 2:1, NKJV). "Has not the Scripture said that the Christ comes from the seed of David and from the town of Bethlehem, where David was?" (John 7:42, NKJV; see Micah 5:1).

He would be born of a virgin — "Now in the sixth month the angel Gabriel was sent by God to a city of Galilee named Nazareth, to a virgin betrothed to a man whose name was Joseph, of the house of David. The virgin's name was Mary. . . . Then the angel said to her, 'Do not be afraid, Mary, for you have found favor with God. And behold, you will conceive in your womb and bring forth a Son, and shall call His name JESUS'" (Luke 1:26-31, NKJV; see Isa. 7:14).

His way would be prepared by a forerunner — "And he went into all the region around the Jordan, preaching a baptism of repentance for the remission of sins, as it is written in the book of the words of Isaiah the prophet, saying: 'The voice of one crying in the wilderness: "Prepare the way of the Lord, make His paths straight. Every valley shall be filled and every mountain and hill brought low; and the crooked places shall be made straight and the rough ways made smooth; and all flesh shall see the salvation of God"'" (Luke 3:3-6, NKJV).

"When the messengers of John had departed, He began to speak to the multitudes concerning John: 'What did you go out into the wilderness to see? A reed shaken by the wind? . . . This is he of whom it is written: "Behold, I send My messenger before Your face, who will prepare Your way before You"'" (Luke 7:24-27, NKJV; see Mal. 3:1).

He would be called the Son of God — "And suddenly a voice came from heaven, saying, 'This is My beloved Son, in whom I am well pleased'" (Matt. 3:17, NKJV; see Ps. 2:7).

His ministry would be in Galilee — "And leaving Nazareth, He came and dwelt in Capernaum, which is by the sea, in the regions of Zebulun and Naphtali, that it might be fulfilled which was spoken by Isaiah the prophet [Isa. 9:1, 2] saying: 'The land of Zebulun and the land of Naphtali, the way of the sea, beyond the Jordan, Galilee of the Gentiles: the people who sat in darkness saw a great light, and upon those who sat in the region and shadow of death light has dawned' [Isa. 9:1, 2]" (Matt. 4:13-16, NKJV).

He would be called a prophet — "And that He may send

Jesus Christ, who was preached to you before. . . . For Moses truly said to the fathers, 'The Lord your God will raise up for you a Prophet like me from your brethren. Him you shall hear in all things, whatever He says to you'" (Acts 3:20-22, NKJV; Matt. 21:11; see Deut. 18:15, 18).

He would heal the brokenhearted—"The Spirit of the Lord is upon Me, because He has anointed Me to preach the gospel to the poor. He has sent Me to heal the brokenhearted, to preach deliverance to the captives and recovery of sight to the blind, to set at liberty those who are oppressed, to preach the acceptable year of the Lord" (Luke 4:18, 19, NJKV; see Isa. 11:1-10; 61:1-3; Ps. 46:7, 8).

He would be rejected by His own people, the Jews— "He came to His own, and His own did not receive Him" (John 1:11, NKJV). "And they all cried out at once, saying, 'Away with this Man, and release to us Barabbas'" (Luke 23:18, NKJV; see Isa. 53:3).

He would be a priest after the order of Melchizedek— "So also Christ did not glorify Himself to become High Priest, but it was He who said to Him: 'You are My Son, today I have begotten You.' As He also says in another place: 'You are a priest forever according to the order of Melchizedek'" (Heb. 5:5, 6, NKJV; cf. Heb. 7:1-28; see Ps. 110:4).

He would come in the name of the Lord—"Then they brought the colt to Jesus and threw their garments on it, and He sat on it. . . . Then those who went before and those who followed cried out, saying: 'Hosanna! "Blessed is He who comes in the name of the Lord!"'" (Mark 11:7-9, NKJV; cf. Matt. 21:6-11; see Zech. 9:9).

He would not be believed—"But although He had done so many signs before them, they did not believe in Him, that the word of Isaiah the prophet might be fulfilled, which he spoke: 'Lord, who has believed our report? And to whom has the arm of the Lord been revealed?'" (John 12:37, 38, NKJV; see Isa. 53:1-3).

He would not answer His accusers—"Then Pilate asked Him again, saying, 'Do You answer nothing? See how many things they testify against You!' But Jesus still answered nothing, so that Pilate marveled" (Mark 15:4, 5, NKJV; see Isa. 53:7).

He would be sacrificed for our sins—"For when we were still without strength, in due time Christ died for the ungodly. . . . But God demonstrates His own love toward us, in that while we were still sinners, Christ died for us" (Rom. 5:6-8, NKJV; see Isa. 53:5).

He would be crucified with criminals—"With Him they also crucified two robbers, one on His right and the other on His left. So the Scripture was fulfilled which says, 'And He was numbered with the transgressors'" (Mark 15:27, 28, NKJV; see Isa. 53:9, 12).

His body would be pierced—"Then He said to Thomas, 'Reach your finger here, and look at My hands; and reach your hand here, and put it into My side. Do not be unbelieving, but believing'" (John 20:27, NKJV; see Zech. 12:10).

He would be scorned and mocked—"And the people stood looking on. But even the rulers with them sneered, saying, 'He saved others; let Him save Himself if He is the Christ, the chosen of God'" (Luke 23:35, NKJV; see Ps. 22:7, 8).

He would pray for His enemies—"Then Jesus said, 'Father, forgive them, for they do not know what they do.' And they divided His garments and cast lots" (verse 34, NKJV; see Isa. 53:12).

Others would gamble for His clothing—"They crucified Him, and divided His garments, casting lots, that it might be fulfilled which was spoken by the prophet: 'They divided My garments among them, and for My clothing they cast lots.' Sitting down, they kept watch over Him there" (Matt. 27:35, 36, NKJV; cf. John 19:23, 24; see Ps. 22:17, 18).

He would feel abandoned by God—"And about the ninth hour Jesus cried out with a loud voice, saying, 'Eli, Eli, lama sabachthani?' that is, 'My God, My God, why have You forsaken Me?'" (verse 46, NKJV; see Ps. 22:1).

His side would be pierced—"But one of the soldiers pierced His side with a spear, and immediately blood and water came out" (John 19:34, NKJV; see Zech. 12:10).

He would be buried with the rich—"Now when evening had come, there came a rich man from Arimathea, named Joseph, who himself had also become a disciple of Jesus. This man went to Pilate and asked for the body of Jesus. Then Pilate commanded the body to be given to him. And when Joseph had taken the body, he wrapped it in a clean linen cloth, and laid it in his new tomb which he had hewn out of the rock; and he rolled a large stone against the door of the tomb, and departed" (Matt. 27:57-61, NKJV; cf. Mark 15:42-45; see Isa. 53:9).

He would be resurrected—"But he said to them, 'Do not be alarmed. You seek Jesus of Nazareth, who was crucified. He is risen! He is not here. See the place where they laid Him. But go and tell His disciples—and Peter—that He is going before you into Galilee; there you will see Him, as He said to you'" (Mark 16:6, 7, NKJV; cf. Luke 24:1-9; Acts 2:32; 1 Cor. 15:4-8; see Isa. 26:19; Hosea 6:2).

He would ascend to God—"So then, after the Lord had

spoken to them, He was received up into heaven, and sat down at the right hand of God" (verse 19, NKJV).

"Therefore He says: 'When He ascended on high, He led captivity captive, and gave gifts to men'" (Eph. 4:8, NKJV; see Ps. 68:18).

Speaking to the men of Israel on the Day of Pentecost, when all the apostles of Y'shua had come into spiritual unity and were filled with the Holy Spirit, the apostle Peter explained how Jesus of Nazareth fulfilled the prophecies of the Holy Scriptures:

"Men of Israel, hear these words: Jesus of Nazareth, a Man attested by God to you by miracles, wonders, and signs which God did through Him in your midst, as you yourselves also know—Him, being delivered by the determined counsel and foreknowledge of God, you have taken by lawless hands, have crucified, and put to death; whom God raised up, having loosed the pains of death, because it was not possible that He should be held by it.

"For David says concerning Him: 'I foresaw the Lord always before my face, for He is at my right hand, that I may not be shaken; therefore my heart rejoiced, and my tongue was glad; moreover my flesh will also rest in hope, because You will not leave my soul in Hades, nor will You allow Your Holy One to see corruption. You have made known to me the ways of life; You will make me full of joy in Your presence.' . . .

"For David did not ascend into the heavens, but he says himself: 'The Lord said to my Lord, "Sit at My right hand, till I make Your enemies Your footstool."'

"Therefore let all the house of Israel know assuredly that God has made this Jesus, whom you crucified, both Lord and Christ" (Acts 2:22-36, NKJV).

Orthodox Jews still await the coming of the Messiah, however. Israeli members of the large and powerful Hasidic movement Habad are convinced that at any moment the Redeemer will arrive in Jerusalem. They have erected yellow billboards across Israel instructing passersby to "Prepare for the Coming of the Messiah." Bumper stickers carry the same message, as do electrified signs atop Habad cars.*

And who is this Messiah they are expecting? Menachem Mendel Schneerson, an aged rabbi from Brooklyn, New York. With an estimated number of followers of between 30,000 and 100,000 around the world, messianic passions among the Habad are beginning to take on the kinds of sentiment as surrounded Jesus Christ when His disciples announced His Messiahship.

Many Jews have expressed anger at the Habad's pronouncements about Schneerson. Other rabbis state caution that the anointing of a Messiah is up to God, and if this man is the Messiah, it will bear out in the end.**

Their comments remind one of the statements made in Acts 5:34-39, when the chief priests of Jesus' day brought Peter and the apostles to their council to reprimand them for teaching in His name. "Then one in the council stood up, a Pharisee named Gamaliel, a teacher of the law held in respect by all the people, and commanded them to put the apostles outside for a little while.

"And he said to them: 'Men of Israel, take heed to yourselves what you intend to do regarding these men. For some time ago Theudas rose up, claiming to be somebody. A number of men, about four hundred, joined him. He was slain, and all who obeyed him were scattered and came to nothing. After this man, Judas of Galilee rose up in the days of the census, and drew away many people after him. He also perished, and all who obeyed him were dispersed.

"'And now I say to you, keep away from these men and let them alone; for if this plan or this work is of men, it will come to nothing; but if it is of God, you cannot overthrow it—lest you even be found to fight against God'" (NKJV).

Jesus' Messiahship has fulfilled Gamaliel's test. His life alone fulfilled the predictions of prophecy.

Time, Mar. 23, 1992.

**Rabbi Schneerson died June 12, 1994, at the age of 92. His death brought great disappointment to those who had hoped he would be the Messiah.

9

The Lamb of God

In the biblical world, people ratified important covenants or agreements between God and man by shedding the blood of certain animals. Until the time of Christ's death, they considered no covenant as really sealed without such shedding of blood.

God tested Abraham's willingness to obey Him by telling him to offer his son Isaac as a sacrifice on an altar on Mount Moriah. When God saw the patriarch's willingness to do so, He immediately provided a ram as a substitute for Isaac. This foreshadowed things to come, for our heavenly Father in the distant future would permit His only Son Jesus (Y'shua) to be offered as the sinless sacrifice, the Lamb of God without blemish, to atone for our sins.

Let's look at the Passover (*Pesach*). Passover is commonly known as the Festival of Freedom. The present Jewish method of observance differs vastly from the manner in which the ancients celebrated it.

In order to grasp the full significance of the Passover and its profound and sublime symbolism, it is necessary to study the Lord's directions recorded in Holy Writ. In the celebration of the Passover feast, the most essential feature was the Passover lamb. Before God carried out the divine decree against the firstborn of Egypt, He told Moses to gather everyone in the community of Israel together. The Lord explained to Moses and Aaron that He was creating a new calendar. "This month shall be your beginning of months; it shall be the first month of the year to you." This tells us that something momentous is about to happen. Later God's people called the month Nisan.

Moses and Aaron instructed each family to take a lamb from their flocks. The lamb had to be perfect, the best male of their flock—"without spot or blemish." They were to remove it from the other sheep and goats on the tenth day of the month and keep it separate and in a safe place until the evening of the fourteenth day. The members of the household were to consume the lamb in one meal. But God said that if the household contained too few family members to consume a whole lamb at one meal, then they should share it with neighbors.

The lamb was to be slaughtered at twilight and its blood placed on the wood around the doorways of their houses. The lamb was to be roasted whole and eaten in its entirety along with unleavened bread and bitter herbs that same night. Nothing was to remain over.

God was very specific in His instructions because He knew what plans He had for the Israelites. He told them that when they ate their meal, they should be dressed to travel. This meal—this lamb—was to be a Passover offering to the Lord.

THE LAMB OF GOD

A Passover offering. Here was something new. The Israelites were familiar with making offerings to the Lord to atone for their sins against God, but this was something that they were not familiar with. What did it mean?

God explained to Moses and Aaron that placing the blood around the doorposts and the beam above the doorway would symbolize that His people were in those houses. He would therefore pass over those houses and spare the occupants of any plaque or harm when God took out His wrath on Egypt.

The people were to forever remember this act on God's part. He said in verses 13-15: "This day shall be to you one of remembrance: you shall celebrate it a festival."

Further, God instructed Moses and Aaron to tell the Israelites that the lamb was to be eaten inside the house. No one was to take any part of it outside to eat it. And, the next utterance is also significant. God said, "Nor shall you break a bone of it" (verse 46).

"Speak to the whole community of Israel and say that on the tenth of this month each of them shall take a lamb to a family, a lamb to a household. But if the household is too small for a lamb, let him share one with a neighbor who dwells nearby, in proportion to the number of persons: you shall contribute for the lamb according to what each household will eat. Your lamb shall be without blemish, a yearling male; you may take it from the sheep or from the goats. You shall keep watch over it until the fourteenth day of this month; and all the assembled congregation of the Israelites shall slaughter it at twilight. They shall take some of the blood and put it on the two doorposts and the lintel of the houses in which they are to eat it. They shall eat the flesh that same night; they shall eat it roasted over the fire, with unleavened bread and with bitter herbs" (Ex. 12:3-9).

"This is how you shall eat it: your loins girded, your sandals on your feet, and your staff in your hand; and you shall eat it hurriedly: it is a passover offering to the Lord" (verses 11, 12).

"And the blood on the houses where you are staying shall be a sign for you: when I see the blood I will pass over you, so that no plague will destroy you when I strike the land of Egypt.

"This day shall be to you one of remembrance: you shall celebrate it a festival to the Lord throughout the ages; you shall celebrate it as an institution for all time. Seven days you shall eat unleavened bread; on the very first day you shall remove leaven from your houses, for whoever eats leavened bread from the first day to the seventh day, that person shall be cut off from Israel" (verses 13-15).

"It [the lamb] shall be eaten in one house; you shall not take any of the flesh outside the house; nor shall you break a bone of it" (verse 46).

By obeying God's ordinance, Israel gave evidence of their faith in the great deliverance that He would accomplish for them. They had to do something to secure the safety of their own firstborn children. The blood on their houses symbolized divine protection for Israel.

Israel became a free people—rescued by God Himself. Their gratitude and faith later found expression in the triumphant anthem of thanksgiving recorded in Exodus 15. This song, which commemorates the great deliverance of the Hebrew people, testifies that God is the hope of all who trust in Him.

For several centuries the observance of Israel's annual feasts centered in wherever its portable sanctuary was located. But after the construction of the first Temple, during the reign of King Solomon (961-920 B.C.E.), Jerusalem became the designated place (1 Kings 11:36).

God required the shedding of innocent blood to teach Israel a lesson of fundamental importance that He could not have conveyed to them by any better method. And that is why on Yom Kippur, the Day of Atonement, the high priest would take the atoning blood of the goat slain as a sin offering for the people and "sprinkle it on the mercy seat and before the mercy seat [i.e., the cover of the ark]" (Lev. 16:15, NKJV). Inside the ark of the covenant rested the two tables of stone upon which God had written His moral law of Ten Commandments with His own finger. The violation of any precept of that law was sin, and the penalty for transgression was death. The sprinkling of the blood of the animal slain as the sin offering for the people signified that it had died symbolically to pay the penalty for their transgression of that sacred law inside the ark.

"Consider, all lives are Mine; the life of the parent and the life of the child are both Mine. The person who sins, only he shall die" (Eze. 18:4).

"Everyone is dross, altogether foul; there is none who does good, not even one" (Ps. 53:4).

"When they sin against You—for there is no man who does not sin" (1 Kings 8:46; cf. 2 Chron. 6:36).

"For there is not one good man on earth who does what is best and doesn't err" (Eccl. 7:20).

"For the wages of sin is death, but the gift of God is eternal life in Christ Jesus our Lord" (Rom. 6:23, NKJV).

If God had not provided a sacrifice for us, we would all be depressed and in hopeless despair. But He made available a way to repent. "For the life of the flesh is in the blood, and I have assigned it to you for making expiation for your lives upon the altar; it is the blood, as life, that effects expiation" (Lev. 17:11).

Centuries before the birth of Christ, the offering of lambs and some other innocent animals as sacrifices foreshadowed His death to provide atonement for sinners. These rites served prophetically to illustrate God's plan of salvation for repentant human beings.

For this purpose, God gave His sinless Son, the Messiah, the innocent Lamb of God, to be our atoning sacrifice, our substitute, as Isaiah 53 so dramatically predicted.

Seven centuries passed before the prophecy recorded by Isaiah came to pass. The early Jewish believers in Jesus considered Him to be the fulfillment of the Passover lambs sacrificed at the annual festival.

Paul, a Hebrew Christian who had studied closely with Rabbi Gamaliel, wrote in 1 Corinthians 5:7: "For indeed Christ, our Passover, was sacrificed for us" (NKJV). The Gospel of John noted that when Jesus died, "it was the Preparation Day of the Passover, and about the sixth hour" (John 19:14, NKJV). This places the time of Jesus' crucifixion at the same time as the slaughtering of the Passover lambs. And verse 31 says that the Jews asked Pilate that the legs of Jesus and the two thieves might be broken so that they might die more quickly. (Crucifixion was a slow and lingering death, and breaking the legs would hasten death because the victims could no longer push themselves up in an attempt to breathe.) But when the soldiers came to break the legs of Jesus, they discovered that He was already dead and thus they did not need to shatter His leg bones to hasten His demise. Jesus, our Passover Lamb, was the perfect sacrifice

THE LAMB OF GOD

for our sins. He was an unblemished offering—the Messiah, the Lamb of God, who brought us out of slavery to freedom, saving us from our sins and giving us redemption.

10

The Jewishness of Jesus

Jesus of Nazareth fulfilled all the criteria set down in the Scriptures for the Messiah. He was born, lived, and died a Jew. While He lived, many of those whom He came to save vilified Him, and even today some Jews continue to do so as we enter the second millennium following His crucifixion. Some even dispute the fact that He ever existed at all.

As I talk with my fellow Jews, I detect a mental block against even thinking about Jesus. I witnessed this phenomenon within my own extended family. It seems that if you express a belief that Jesus is the Messiah, you become a traitor to the Jewish faith. It appears that one must deny Y'shua to maintain one's Jewish identity. Or if one professes to be a Christian, you must deny the Jewishness of Christ. But scholars (both Christian and Jewish) and many others are increasingly recognizing the complete Jewishness of

Jesus and His early followers.

Society seems to demand that we choose one faith or the other—Jew or Christian. If we don't, people cannot put a finger on us or cubbyhole us into neat little boxes if we both keep the commandments and have the testimony of Jesus. Why then do so many of us of Jewish ethnic origin seem to be able to transcend these barriers—these rigid stances that keep our people from receiving the blessings that YHWH wishes to bestow upon us?

Truth can be found only in the whole Testament—the entire Bible consisting of both the Old and New Testaments. If you are a Christian, do not deny yourself all the truths contained in the Holy Scriptures, for they provide the very foundation upon which your religious teachings are based. To know Jesus, you must study the Scriptures, as He said, remembering that the only Scriptures that Jesus knew were those written prior to His birth. His Holy Scriptures are what the Christian world refers to as the Old Testament.

To my fellow Jews, I invite, encourage, and entreat you to open the pages of the New Testament. Study with an open but probing mind. Read the good news that the apostles embraced. You will be surprised that each chapter speaks directly to us Jews. To believe that Y'shua is the Messiah foretold by the ancients in Holy Writ does not make you a traitor to your faith. You are not breaking the covenant with YHWH. Instead, you are fulfilling it—you are truly becoming a member of the tribe by choosing to claim the promises of the new covenant.

I studied with rabbis throughout my young adulthood, searching for the answers to life's meaning. Somehow, the words of Isaiah, Jeremiah, Micah, and the other prophets that spoke of the long-awaited coming of the Messiah did not enter our discussions. When I asked why so many believed that Jesus Christ is the Messiah, the responses I received were not scriptural. But I pressed on. I wanted to know, and I continued to search the Scriptures for answers every day.

The Bible contains a world of wisdom, yet until recently it was too often beyond the abilities of the average person to understand. The translations from the Greek, Aramaic, and Hebrew into English were archaic. Only the most dedicated and inspired could wade through the language, comprehending only parts of what they read. Today the Bible is available in a wide variety of formats—the printed word, computer diskettes, pictures, cassette tapes, and videos. Even in the most remote regions, satellite television technology can bring religious programming to those who wish to avail themselves of it.

The Holy Scripture focuses on the history of the people Israel and their anticipation of the coming of the Messiah. The New Testament reveals the fulfillment of those prophecies and details the life and times of the Messiah, *Y'shua' ha-Mashiach*, or in English, Jesus Christ.

The first book of the New Testament, the Gospel of Matthew, documents the genealogy of Jesus Christ, the Son of David, the Son of Abraham. His human parents, Joseph and Mary, were betrothed when he discovered she was pregnant. In those days (and not so many years ago even now), to become pregnant without full benefit of marriage (betrothal was considered only partial marriage) was a major offense. Mary could have been stoned for such an indiscretion.

Does the Bible say that Jesus was conceived out of wedlock and considered to be illegitimate, as so many critics claim? Some scholars contend that was the case. But Scripture has another answer that may seem difficult to grasp, but for many Christians is a major doctrine of their faith.

"Joseph her husband, being a just man, and not wanting to make her a public example, was minded to put her away secretly. But while he thought about these things, behold, an angel of the Lord appeared to him in a dream, saying, 'Joseph, son of David, do not be afraid to take to you Mary your wife, for that which is conceived in her is of the Holy Spirit. And she will bring forth a Son, and you shall call His name Jesus, for He will save His people from their sins'" (Matt. 1:19-21, NKJV).

The name "Jesus" comes from the Greek *Iesous*, which is a transliteration of the Aramaic *Yeshua*, taken from the Hebrew word *Yehoshua*, or Joshua, meaning "YHWH is salvation." The word *Christ* is transliterated from the Greek *Christos*, corresponding to the Hebrew *Mashiach*, or Messiah, meaning "anointed or anointed one." When Jesus lived on earth, His parents no doubt called Him by His Hebrew name. Jewish believers, then, would have referred to Him as *Y'shua' ha-Mashiach*. Through the translations and transliterations from Hebrew to Aramaic to Greek to English, therefore, the names Jesus Christ spoken together as one unit have come to mean Jesus the Saviour, the Messiah, the Son of God.

But what of the prophesy in Isaiah 7:14 that declared: "Assuredly, my Lord will give you a sign of His own accord! Look, the young woman is with child and about to give birth to a son. Let her name him *Immanuel* ['God with us']." As we have seen in the previous chapters on the names of God and His Son, both the heavenly Father and His Son have had many names, their purpose being to describe attributes such as character. Immanuel, "God with us," records the divine nature of the Saviour.

Jesus' parents were not the only ones to whom the angel of the Lord stated that He would be of special significance to the Jewish people. The Wise Men from the East came to Jerusalem after His birth and asked, "Where is He who has been born King of the Jews? For we have seen His star in the East and have come to worship Him" (Matt. 2:2, NKJV).

Their question disturbed the reigning king, Herod. Scripture had foretold the day of the Messiah, so not only Herod but the Jewish people expected His eventual arrival. Afraid of losing his power and might to this Messiah, Herod deceitfully told the Wise Men to locate the young Child and bring word to him so that he could "come and worship Him also" (verse 8, NKJV).

The men went on their way, and again the "star which they had seen in the East went before them, till it came and stood over where the young Child was. When they saw the star, they rejoiced with exceedingly great joy. And when they had come into the house, they saw the young Child with Mary His mother, and fell down and worshiped Him. And when they had opened their treasures, they presented gifts to Him: gold, frankincense, and myrrh" (verses 9-11, NKJV).

God continued to place His loving protection over Jesus. Again His angels issued a warning on His behalf. "Then, being divinely warned in a dream that they [the Wise Men] should not return to Herod, they departed for their own country another way. Now when they had departed, behold, an angel of the Lord appeared to Joseph in a dream, saying, 'Arise, take the young Child and His mother, flee to Egypt, and stay there until I bring you word; for Herod will seek the young Child to destroy Him.' When he arose, he took the young Child and His mother by night and departed for

Egypt, and was there until the death of Herod, that it might be fulfilled which was spoken by the Lord through the prophet, saying, 'Out of Egypt I called My Son' [Hosea 11:1]" (verses 12-15, NKJV).

Herod, who realized he'd been deceived by the Wise Men, issued a diabolical death decree for all male children in Bethlehem and its surrounding districts 2 years old and under, hoping to kill the young Christ at the same time. But as we know, the One who was to become the Saviour of humanity escaped.

The angel of the Lord had also come to the shepherds tending their flocks near Bethlehem. "Then the angel said to them, 'Do not be afraid, for behold, I bring you good tidings of great joy which will be to all people. For there is born to you this day in the city of David a Savior, who is Christ the Lord. And this will be the sign to you: You will find a Babe wrapped in swaddling cloths, lying in a manger.' And suddenly there was with the angel a multitude of the heavenly host praising God and saying: 'Glory to God in the highest, and on earth peace, good will toward men!'" (Luke 2:10-14, NKJV).

Luke records that those who knew the Scriptures received Jesus. After the shepherds visited with Mary, Joseph, and Jesus, they praised God for all the things they had heard and seen.

And since Jesus was born a Jew, He was circumcised on the eighth day following His birth, in keeping with the ancient covenant. Later Joseph and Mary took Him to Jerusalem "to present Him to the Lord (as it is written in the law of the Lord, 'Every male who opens the womb shall be called holy to the Lord' [see Ex. 13:2, 12, 15])" (Luke 2:22, 23, NKJV). His parents offered a sacrifice on His behalf of a pair of turtledoves, or two young pigeons (Lev. 12:8).

While the family was in Jerusalem they met a man by the name of Simeon, whom Scripture describes as being "just and devout, waiting for the Consolation of Israel, and the Holy Spirit was upon him. And it had been revealed to him by the Holy Spirit that he would not see death before he had seen the Lord's Christ [Messiah]. So he came by the Spirit into the temple. And when the parents brought in the Child Jesus, to do for Him according to the custom of the law, he took Him up in his arms and blessed God and said: 'Lord, now You are letting Your servant depart in peace, according to Your word; for my eyes have seen Your salvation which You have prepared before the face of all peoples, a light to bring revelation to the Gentiles, and the glory of Your people Israel' [see Isa. 9:2; 42:6]. . . .

"Then Simeon blessed them, and said to Mary His mother, 'Behold, this Child is destined for the fall and rising of many in Israel, and for a sign which will be spoken against (yes, a sword will pierce through your own soul also) that the thoughts of many hearts may be revealed'" (Luke 2:26-35, NKJV).

Not only did Simeon welcome and praise the arrival of the Messiah, but also the prophetess Anna, an elderly widow who lived at the Temple, serving God with fasting and prayers night and day. When she saw Jesus, she gave thanks to the Lord and spoke of Him to all who looked for redemption in Jerusalem.

You can see from the beginning that not only Joseph and Mary recognized that Jesus was the Messiah, but others did as well.

Jesus grew up in much the same way my father did, learning Hebrew, studying the Scriptures, memorizing prayers, keeping the Sabbath holy by attending services in the synagogue, as well as eating kosher (ceremonially clean) foods as prescribed by Mosaic law. Being a Jewish boy, He followed the rites of passage into Jewish manhood, at the age of 12 studying to become Bar Mitzvah in preparation for taking His place with the elders in the Jewish community.

Luke 2 speaks of Jesus' childhood. "And the Child grew and became strong in spirit, filled with wisdom; and the grace of God was upon Him. His parents went to Jerusalem every year at the Feast of the Passover. And when He was twelve years old, they went up to Jerusalem according to the custom of the feast.

"When they had finished the days, as they returned, the Boy Jesus lingered behind in Jerusalem. And Joseph and His mother did not know it; but supposing Him to have been in the company, they went a day's journey, and sought Him among their relatives and acquaintances. So when they did not find Him, they returned to Jerusalem, seeking Him.

"Now so it was that after three days they found Him in the temple, sitting in the midst of the teachers, both listening to them and asking them questions. And all who heard Him were astonished at His understanding and answers. So when they saw Him, they were amazed; and His mother said to Him, 'Son, why have You done this to us? Look, Your father and I have sought You anxiously.'

"And He said to them, 'Why is it that you sought Me? Did you not know that I must be about My Father's business?' But they did not understand the statement which He spoke to them" (verses 40-50, NKJV).

When I first read these words, being the parent of a teenager, I felt Jesus was being impertinent. Perhaps His parents did also. Yet it also shows that Jesus, even as a child, was aware of His mission in life, and perhaps He wondered why—with all the signs that His parents had received since His birth—they still did not understand.

He returned to Nazareth with His parents, and as the Bible says, "was subject to them" while Mary kept all the things that He said and that happened to Him "in her heart" (verse 51, NKJV). She continued to see God's purpose being fulfilled in this special Son of theirs. And while He grew, "Jesus increased in wisdom and stature, and in favor with God and men" (verse 52, NKJV).

Jesus' special purpose—His ministry—became recognized when John the Baptist began baptizing people in the Jordan. He said: "I indeed baptize you with water unto repentance, but He who is coming after me is mightier than I, whose sandals I am not worthy to carry. He will baptize you with the Holy Spirit and fire" (Matt. 3:11, NKJV).

When Jesus arrived from Galilee to John at the Jordan to be baptized by him, John protested: "I have need to be baptized by You, and are You coming to me?" (verse 14, NKJV).

But Jesus convinced him to do it. And after He came up out of the water, "behold, the heavens were opened to Him, and He saw the Spirit of God descending like a dove and alighting upon Him" (verse 16, NKJV). It was just as had been foretold in Isaiah 11:2. Luke described the Holy Spirit as descending "in bodily form like a dove" (Luke 3:22, NKJV).

"And suddenly a voice came from heaven, saying, 'This is My beloved Son, in whom I am well pleased'" (Matt. 3:17, NKJV). "This is My servant, whom I uphold. My chosen one, in whom I delight. I have put My Spirit upon him" (Isa. 42:1).

A number of religious leaders, considering Him to be blasphemous by speaking and teaching with the authority belonging only to God, harassed Jesus on all sides. They could not and would not see the spirit of holiness that was in Him, and they challenged Him. They feared, too, that He would usurp their own authority. Comfortable with the status quo, they didn't want it disrupted. This sounds like an indictment, yet at the same time I can understand their confusion and annoyance.

But Jesus sought to assure them that it was not His purpose to start up a new religion, but to call the Jewish people back to God (YHWH), His heavenly Father. "Do not think that I came to destroy the Law or the Prophets. I did not come to destroy but to fulfill. For assuredly, I say to you, till heaven and earth pass away, one jot or one tittle will by no means pass from the law till all is fulfilled. Whoever therefore breaks one of the least of these commandments, and teaches men so, shall be called least in the kingdom of heaven; but whoever does and teaches them, he shall be called great in the kingdom of heaven. For I say to you, that unless your righteousness exceeds the righteousness of the scribes and Pharisees, you will by no means enter the kingdom of heaven" (Matt. 5:17-20, NKJV).

He urged the people of Israel as well as their religious leaders to stop speaking empty words and to stop doing things to bring honor upon themselves rather than for the good that would come from their deeds. He was reminding the people of Israel to return to their high calling—their covenant to be a nation of priests—and to take their light and let it shine throughout the world. Not for their own sakes, but for every nation and creed. Everything He did and said was to uplift God and instill within humanity a genuine love for one another.

Jesus instructed His disciples: "Do not go into the way of

131

the Gentiles, and do not enter a city of the Samaritans, but go rather to the lost sheep of the house of Israel" (Matt. 10:5, 6, NKJV). They were to deliver their message first to them.

John the Baptist, when he saw Jesus approaching him for baptism, said: "Behold! The Lamb of God who takes away the sin of the world! This is He of whom I said, 'After me comes a Man who is preferred before me, for He was before me.' I did not know Him; but that He should be revealed to Israel, therefore I came baptizing with water" (John 1:29-31, NKJV). Afterward John announced: "I have seen and testified that this is the Son of God" (verse 34, NKJV). Later that day, while standing with two of his disciples, he looked at Jesus and said again: "Behold the Lamb of God!" (verse 36, NKJV).

The two disciples called Jesus "rabbi" (teacher). One of them whose name was Andrew told his brother: "'We have found the Messiah' (which is translated, the Christ)" (verse 41, NKJV). The following day Philip, another disciple, went to Nathanael and said to him: "We have found Him of whom Moses in the law, and also the prophets, wrote—Jesus of Nazareth, the son of Joseph" (verse 45, NKJV).

"There was a man of the Pharisees named Nicodemus, a ruler of the Jews. This man came to Jesus by night and said to Him, 'Rabbi, we know that You are a teacher come from God; for no one can do these signs that You do unless God is with him.'

"Jesus answered and said to him, 'Most assuredly, I say to you, unless one is born again, he cannot see the kingdom of God'" (John 3:1-3, NKJV).

Nicodemus didn't understand what Jesus meant by that. He asked Him: "How can a man be born when he is old? Can he enter a second time into his mother's womb and be born?"

(verse 4, NKJV).

Once again Jesus explained: "Unless one is born of water and the Spirit, he cannot enter the kingdom of God" (verse 5, NKJV). This was Israel's opportunity to be born again. "That which is born of the flesh is flesh, and that which is born of the Spirit is spirit" (verse 6, NKJV).

That God's kingdom was not a physical thing but a spiritual one was a difficult concept even for those who walked closest with Jesus—His disciples. During His last hours on earth, at the Passover celebration in Jerusalem, they still jostled one another to gain favored status so that they would have positions of importance in the human kingdom they expected to emerge.

By washing the feet of the disciples—especially those of Peter—Jesus showed these men who would be responsible for taking His message of love to the world, of demonstrating what true humility was. Here the Son of God, the Messiah, completed a lowly task, one that a servant would have ordinarily performed. For that is what Jesus expected of His disciples—that they would serve humanity as His representatives following His crucifixion.

How supremely appropriate for Jesus to have selected the Passover service to demonstrate how His followers should serve others. It was the memorial to the Exodus, where God (YHWH) had delivered the Jews from the Egyptians. The blood of a sacrificial lamb sprinkled over the doorposts of their houses saved them from certain death. John the Baptist said, "Behold the Lamb of God." Jesus' blood stands above our doorposts. His blood was sacrificed for ours, the oblation for our sins.

Jesus was born, lived, and died a Jew. After He left the

Passover supper, one of His own betrayed Him to the enemy, and they hung Him on the cross to die — not for His sins, but for ours. He died on the eve of the Sabbath, rested in the tomb on the Sabbath, and on Sunday was resurrected. On the cross where He was crucified, Pilate wrote a title and hung it there. It announced: "JESUS OF NAZARETH, THE KING OF THE JEWS" (John 19:19, NKJV) in Hebrew, Greek, and Latin so that all could see. Yes, it is true. He is the King of the Jews, the King of kings.

In his account of Jesus' life, the apostle John wrote: "This is the disciple who testifies of these things, and wrote these things; and we know that his testimony is true. And there are also many other things that Jesus did, which if they were written one by one, I suppose that even the world itself could not contain the books that would be written. Amen" (John 21:24, 25, NKJV).

I heartily agree. The New Testament contains 27 books recording the life and teachings of Jesus Christ from the unique perspectives of His disciples, showing both His humanity and deity. It documents the accounts of the struggles of the apostles after the resurrection of Jesus and tells of the spread of the early Christian churches that contained a mixture of Jews and Gentiles.

Did the Jewish people accept Y'shua as their Messiah? People joined the church daily, the Word says (Acts 2:47; 5:14). Most of those were Jews, including many Pharisees and Sadducees — persons who comprised the very elect in the Jewish religious hierarchy (Acts 6:7). The apostles were themselves Jews, as were all the writers of the New Testament except for Luke, a Gentile referred to as the "beloved physician" (Col. 4:14, NKJV). Thus many of His own people proclaimed Him as their Messiah.

11

People of the Covenant

"Thus said God the Lord,
 Who created the heavens and stretched them out,
 Who spread out the earth and what it brings forth,
 Who gave breath to the people upon it
 And life to those who walk thereon:
 I the Lord, in My grace, have summoned you,
 And I have grasped you by the hand.
 I created you, and appointed you
 A covenant people —a light of nations —
 Opening eyes deprived of light,
 Rescuing prisoners from confinement
 From the dungeon those who sit in darkness.
 I am the Lord, that is My name;
 I will not yield My glory to another" (Isa. 42:5-8).

The relationship between God and the people of Israel is described as being covenantal. As we have seen before, *covenant* implies a pact, an agreement between individuals in which stipulations are accepted by one or both parties and then considered binding upon both parties (i.e., a legal contract such as a marriage agreement could be considered a covenant).

The ancient world knew of two kinds of covenants—one between those of equal stature, and another between lord and vassal, conqueror and conquered, superior and inferior. In the latter case, the lord and conqueror stipulated the conditions, privileges, and responsibilities accruing to both parties, and the vassal or subject nation submitted to the conditions imposed on it.

In Genesis 21:22-32, for example, the patriarch Abraham made a covenant with King Abimelech of Gerar in which the two men swore an oath that they would not deal falsely with one another. To seal the pact, Abraham took sheep and oxen and gave them to Abimelech. The place where the pact took place came to be called Beersheba ("the well of swearing seven"), for there the two of them swore an oath.

But in the case of a covenant between God and human beings, obviously God the superior determined the conditions and provisions of the agreement, made them known to His people, and gave them the choice of accepting or rejecting the covenant. Once ratified, however, it was considered binding upon both God and His people.

When God placed Adam in the Garden of Eden, He told him, "Of every tree of the garden you are free to eat; but as for the tree of knowledge of good and bad, you must not eat of it; for as soon as you eat of it, you shall die" (Gen. 2:16). It was a commandment from God to Adam—an order—and He expected him to comply. And though other writers have stated that it was the first covenant between God and humanity in Scripture, I do not read anywhere that Adam verbally assented to be bound by this order from his Creator or that he was even free to do so at this point in time. However, one could assume that in this instance it represented a covenant between lord and vassal.

Yet we can see a deeply loving and caring relationship between God and His creation, Adam, like a father for a son. It is evident in verse 18, where God says: "It is not good for man to be alone; I will make a fitting helper for him." So God cast a sleep upon Adam during which He prepared a mate for him from his own bones. Upon being presented with this woman, Adam expressed his appreciation by declaring: "This one at last is bone of my bones and flesh of my flesh. This one shall be called Woman, for from man was she taken" (verse 23).

Even after Eve succumbed to the lies of the serpent, Satan, and Adam also disobeyed God by eating the fruit from the tree of "knowledge of good and bad," their Maker did not instantly destroy them. He could have simply created another couple to populate our world. Despite His disappointment in Adam and Eve for disobeying His direct order, God still had compassion on them. Instead of immediately requiring their lives, He instead banished them from the Garden of Eden and withdrew His blessing from the ground because of their deeds. Eventually they would die, so God did, in essence, keep His word—"You shall die"—yet it did not happen instantly.

But in the same breath, God told the serpent that He would put enmity, or hostility, between him and the woman and between the serpent's offspring and hers. "They shall strike at [crush] your head, and you shall strike at their heel" (Gen. 3:15). The New King James Version translates the verse using the singular: "He shall bruise your head, and you shall bruise His heel." Traditionally this is taken as a reference to a specific person—someone who would save humanity, i.e., the Messiah.

As a parent I can't help but share the feeling of disappointment that our heavenly Father must have had when He gave His creation the freedom of choice and it was misused. I know my own parents have been disappointed in choices I have made in my life, though they prepared me for such choices by giving me firm instruction. Yet the Lord held back His judgment and kept His distance, allowing Adam and Eve and their offspring to suffer the consequences of their own actions, until things got totally out of hand. How often do we as parents—after stating the rules and laying out the boundaries to our children, and after much hand wringing and heartbreak—throw up our hands and just let things run their course?

Genesis 6 tells us that when the Lord saw how wicked men had become, He decided to erase all living things from the face of the earth. "And the Lord regretted that He had made man on earth, and His heart was saddened" (verse 6).

In my mind I see a heavenly Father who had great hopes for His children, but they have run amok. In Genesis 3 God is the authoritarian—dictating to Adam and Eve the parameters of existence. But though the couple heard Him and knew what was expected of them, they did not make a covenant with Him verbally. Those were simply the rules given to them. They did not assent to it because it was not broached to them in that way.

Many methods of child rearing exist in the world today. One is a totally authoritarian method in which the parents order the child to comply. When I was growing up, children were raised that way—to be seen but not heard, to obey without question. As a parent I have observed other methods—some totally child-centered, while in others the child is given rules as well as the opportunity to participate in the decision-making. No one method works well with all children. Perhaps our heavenly Father, upon seeing that neither the authoritarian method nor allowing them to be left to their own devices worked with Adam and Eve, decided to try another approach by laying out the plan and gaining compliance through negotiation—by entering into an agreement or covenant. This is a popular method even today between parents and teens.

But though God declared He would eliminate both the human beings and beasts He had created on this earth (which initially He found to be good), He did not. Had He done so, none of us would be here today. Scripture says: "Noah found favor with the Lord. . . . Noah was a righteous man; he was blameless in his age; Noah walked with God" (verses 8, 9). So God decided to save Noah, his sons, his wife, and his sons' wives. And because of His love for him, God made a covenant with Noah. Though God was about to destroy everything else on the earth, He would save Noah in the boat God had instructed him to build.

And here is the key. Noah did just as God commanded him, so he entered into the covenant with the Lord. And God kept His part of the bargain. He did just as He had said He would. "All existence on earth was blotted out—man, cattle, creeping things, and birds of the sky. . . . Only Noah was left, and those with him in the ark" (Gen. 7:23).

God had made a covenant of life and death between Himself and Noah. God said: "'For My part, I am about to bring the Flood—waters upon the earth—to destroy all flesh under the sky in which there is breath of life; everything on earth shall perish. But I will establish My covenant with you, and you shall enter the ark, with your sons, your wife, and your sons' wives. And of all that lives, of all flesh, you shall take two of each into the ark to keep alive with you; they shall be male and female. From birds of every kind, cattle of every kind, every kind of creeping thing on earth, two of each shall come to you to stay alive. For your part, take of everything that is eaten and store it away, to serve as food for you and for them.' Noah did so; just as God commanded him, so he did" (Gen. 6:17-22).

After the water subsided, God told him to leave the ark. And Noah immediately built an altar to the Lord and offered sacrifices on it. God then vowed never to destroy the earth in the same way again (Gen. 8:21). He blessed Noah and his sons because of their faithfulness to His previous covenant. And to them He made another covenant—a commitment that would extend to all those who came after them and continued to keep their promise to God.

"And God said to Noah and to his sons with him, 'I now establish My covenant with you and your offspring to come, and with every living thing that is with you—birds, cattle, and every wild beast as well—all that have come out of the ark, every living thing on earth. I will maintain My covenant with you: never again shall all flesh be cut off by the waters of a flood, and never again shall there be a flood to destroy the earth.'

"God further said, 'This is the *sign* that I set *for the covenant* between Me and you, and every living creature with you, for all ages to come. I have set My bow in the clouds, and it shall serve as a *sign of the covenant* between Me and the earth. When I bring clouds over the earth, and the bow appears in the clouds, I will remember My covenant between Me and you and every living creature among all flesh, so that the waters shall never again become a flood to destroy all flesh. . . . That,' God said to Noah, 'shall be the sign of the covenant that I have established *between Me and all flesh that is on earth*'" (Gen. 9:8-17).

Throughout Scripture we read of a continuing covenant between God and man—a covenant with renewed promises.

God made a *covenant of land* with Abram that specified that Israel would belong to the Hebrews forever (Gen. 15:18). He told the patriarch when he was 99 years old that he would father many children if he would keep a covenant with Him. "'Walk in My ways and be blameless. I will establish My covenant between Me and you, and I will make you exceedingly numerous.' Abram threw himself on his face; and God spoke to him further, 'As for Me, this is My covenant with you: You shall be the father of a multitude of nations. And you shall no longer be called Abram, but your name shall be Abraham, for I make you the father of a multitude of nations. I will make you exceedingly fertile, and make nations of you; and kings shall come forth from you. I will maintain My covenant between Me and you, and your offspring to come, as *an everlasting covenant* throughout the ages, *to be God to you and to your offspring to come.* I assign the land you sojourn in to you and your offspring to come, all the land of Canaan, as an everlasting holding. I will be their God'" (Gen. 17:1-7).

The promise God made to Abraham was an everlasting covenant with all succeeding generations, but Abraham had conditions to fulfill for the blessings to take place. Abraham and all his offspring throughout the ages would have to observe the covenant that God had made with Abraham. The sign that this covenant still continued was for all males in the household—children, slaves whether born in the house or purchased from outside—to be circumcised. That was the pact. Male children were to be circumcised eight days following birth. Any male not circumcised would be cut off from his family because he had broken the covenant (see Gen. 17:9-14).

Abram already had a son, Ishmael, who had been born to Hagar, his wife Sarai's slave. When Sarai failed to conceive and bear Abram a son, she had convinced him to take Hagar to bed. Does this sound a little like Eve taking things into her own hands? Abram listened to his wife instead of waiting for God to fulfill His promise to make him the father of many nations. He was weak and probably confused—like so many of us would have been under similar circumstances.

When God told Abraham that He would bless Sarai and give him a son by her, Abraham threw himself down before God on his face and laughed. Abraham was already 100 years old, and Sarai was 90. He thought it was impossible. And without God it would have been. So Abraham, who already had a son whom he loved, said to God: "O that Ishmael might live by Your favor!" (verse 17). He wanted the Lord to include this son in any blessing.

But God said: "Nevertheless, Sarah your wife shall bear you a son, and you shall name him Isaac; and I will maintain My covenant with him as an everlasting covenant for his offspring to come" (verse 19). So God was telling Abraham that the lineage that would receive the special blessing and through whom His covenant would be passed down was that of his son Isaac.

Yet Abraham's pleas for Ishmael did not fall upon deaf ears. God said: "As for Ishmael, I have heeded you. I hereby bless him. I will make him fertile and exceedingly numerous. He shall be the father of twelve chieftains, and I will make of him a great nation. But My covenant I will maintain with Isaac, whom Sarah shall bear to you at this season next year" (verses 20, 21).

The Lord kept His promise to Abraham concerning Ishmael. The lad grew up, lived in the wilderness, and became a bowman, and his mother obtained a wife for him from the land of Egypt (Gen. 21:21). He became the father of the Arab nations. Those who read the prophecy given to his mother, Hagar, in the wilderness will see it has indeed come true. "'I will greatly increase your offspring, and they shall be too many to count. . . . Behold, you are with child and shall bear a son; you shall call him Ishmael, for the Lord has paid heed to your suffering. He shall be a wild ass of a man; his hand against everyone, and everyone's hand against him; he shall dwell alongside of all his kinsmen'" (Gen. 16:10-12).

Abraham met his part of the covenant. That very day he took every male in his household—including Ishmael—and circumcised them as God had told him to do. Abraham was 99 years old when he was circumcised and Ishmael was 13.

Although to us today circumcision might seem a barbaric practice, at that time it was the custom for covenants to be ratified in blood. When God gave the Ten Commandments to the Hebrews, Moses set up an altar at the foot of the mountain and offered burnt offerings. "Moses took one part of the blood and put it in basins, and the other part of the blood he dashed against the altar. Then he took the record of the covenant and read it aloud to the people. And they said, 'All that the Lord has spoken we will faithfully do!' Moses took the blood and dashed it on the people and said, '*This is the blood of the covenant* that the Lord now makes with you concerning all these commands'" (Ex. 24:6-8).

The word covenant in Hebrew is *b'rith.* Even today Jewish parents maintain this blood of the covenant by circumcising their sons in the traditional manner on the eighth day with a ritual ceremony called the "covenant of circumcism *(berit milah),*" or *"bris,"* the Ashkenazi version of the word. My own sons, Ben Daniel and David Scott, were also circumcised on the eighth day by their physicians in accordance with the covenant.

Reading about the relationship between God and humanity throughout Scripture, I can see God looking for a people who will walk in love and righteousness with Him. In Noah and successive generations, He found some who did. But by and large, God recognized that humanity needed something tangible and finite that they could see and touch to remind them of the way in which He wanted them to live and get along with one another. For that reason, He devised the Ten Commandments, calling Moses to the mountaintop, where He personally inscribed on stone tablets His law for healthful living and loving conduct. It was not simply a whim on His part, nor were the commandments He inscribed on stone with His own finger just ordinances that Moses created to try and keep the people under his thumb. They were holy writ — everlasting and unchanging guides to living on our world.

Scripture calls the Ten Commandments *the Two Tablets of the Covenant,* and the holy ark that housed them the *"Ark of the Covenant of the Lord."* The prophet Ezekiel speaks of a *"covenant of friendship," "an everlasting covenant"* between God and the children of Israel (Eze. 34:25; 37:26).

The purpose of the covenants between God and the Israelites was to create a holy people who would live in accordance with His will. And through their living testimony, His Word would spread among the peoples of the world. God had promised that Abraham's seed would bless all humanity.

He made and renewed the covenant with each of the patriarchs. It is explicit and binds the people as a whole as well as each individual personally. It is as valid for us today as it was in ancient times. But because God first made it with the genetic seed of Abraham's line, does it mean that only those who are Abraham's physical descendants are the people of the covenant? The traditional definition of a Jew is a person born of Jewish parents or a convert to Judaism. Such a person possesses both the sanctity of the Jewish people (Ex. 19:6) and the obligation to observe the commandments. Let's see what Scripture says about this question.

Even while Moses was on the mountain with God receiving the Ten Commandments, the people of Israel were reveling in idolatry in camp. How incredible it must have seemed to their leader that they couldn't keep their faith while he was gone for just that short period. As time passed, the people began focusing their worship on the tablets of stone themselves and the ark in which they were carried. What occurred thereafter is a trend that has repeated itself throughout all generations. The manifestations of religion and worship became more important than God and His Word. The ritual and the physical settings took on greater significance than the Creator Himself.

A friend of mine, Lillian Boyer, of Trout Creek, Montana, told me something that I'll pass along to you: "They came to worship the goddess, and stayed to worship the veils." It is such a truism. People come with good intentions to worship the Lord, but somehow the lines become blurred between the worshiping of God Himself and the images (representations, icons, rituals, theologies, etc.) surrounding Him. I always think of this when I see worshipers during the high holy days in the temple rushing to kiss or touch the Torah and in the Catholic Church where the feet of the statues of Jesus and Mary have sometimes been rubbed off by adoring parishioners. I wonder occasionally whether the doing of such rituals has become for many a substitute for real worship.

Recognizing our limitations and imperfections, it is no wonder that our heavenly Father made as the first of the Ten Commandments "You shall not make for yourself a sculptured image, or any likeness of what is in the heavens above, or on the earth below, or in the waters under the earth" (Ex. 20:4). Throughout Scripture God repeatedly asks humanity why it makes things the object of its worship rather than worshiping the Creator Himself.

You'll hear people say that the old covenant has passed away, and we are no longer subject to the law because the new covenant has superseded it. Just read the church listings in the religious section of any newspaper. You'll see that many Christian churches refer to themselves as new covenant churches.

Is it true? Are we no longer bound by the everlasting covenant that Scripture has said is to be kept to the last generation? Are the Ten Commandments really done away with?

What does the Bible say?

Concerning the two covenants, Jeremiah the prophet wrote: "'Behold, the days are coming,' says the Lord, 'when I will make a new covenant with the house of Israel and with the house of Judah—not according to the covenant that I made with their fathers in the day that I took them by the hand to bring them out of the land of Egypt, My covenant which they broke, though I was a husband to them,' says the Lord. 'But this is the covenant that I will make with the house of Israel: After those days, says the Lord, I will put My law in their minds, and write it on their hearts; and I will be their God, and they shall be My people. No more shall every man teach his neighbor, and every man his brother, saying, "Know the Lord," for they all shall know Me, from the least of them to the greatest of them,' says the Lord. 'For I will forgive their iniquity, and their sin I will remember no more'" (Jer. 31:31-34, NKJV).

In essence, the two covenants are the same. Both embody the law of the Ten Commandments. So how do they differ? Under the old covenant that God made with ancient Israel, the ten-commandment law had been engraved by God's finger on two tables of stone, but under the new covenant the *same* ten-commandment law is to be written in the minds and hearts of His faithful believers. But instead of seeing the commandments as rules that had to be kept out of fear of retribution from God, the love inherent in them would be fully understood by His people.

Even in the days of Moses, God had said: "Oh, that they had such an heart in them that they would fear Me and always keep all My commandments, that it might be well with them and with their children forever!" (Deut. 5:29, NKJV).

A covenant is a solemn promise or agreement. The Lord has kept His promise to humanity throughout all generations. It is humanity who has not been faithful.

God said to the ancient patriarch Abraham: "I will maintain My covenant between Me and you, and your offspring to come, as an *everlasting covenant* throughout the ages, to be God to you and to your offspring to come" (Gen. 17:7).

147

Psalm 105:8-10 declares: "He has remembered His covenant forever, the word which He commanded for a thousand generations, the covenant which He made with Abraham, and His oath to Isaac, and confirmed it to Jacob for a statute, to Israel for an everlasting covenant" (NKJV).

What was the nature of the first covenant made with ancient Israel? To know and love our heavenly Father and live our lives in accordance with His will.

Exodus 19:3-6 tells how "Moses went up to God. The Lord called to him from the mountain, saying, 'Thus shall you say to the house of Jacob and declare to the children of Israel: "You have seen what I did to the Egyptians, how I bore you on eagles' wings and brought you to Me. Now then, if you will obey Me faithfully and keep My covenant, you shall be My treasured possession above all the peoples. Indeed, all the earth is Mine, but you shall be to Me a kingdom of priests and a holy nation."'"

This is the covenant God proposed to the Israelites at Mount Sinai. It is the covenant the people agreed to when "all the people answered as one, saying, 'All that the Lord has spoken we will do!'" (verse 8). They made their vow days before God spoke the Ten Commandments on Mount Sinai. "When He finished speaking with him on Mount Sinai, He gave Moses the two tablets of the Pact, stone tablets inscribed with the finger of God" (Ex. 31:18). It is because the people of Israel broke the conditions of the first covenant that God had to renew it, that the "new" one became necessary.

Many Christians today contend that because we are now living under the new covenant, it is no longer necessary to observe the Ten Commandments.

Let us see what the New Testament tells us: "In that He

says, 'A new covenant,' He has made the first obsolete. Now what is becoming obsolete and growing old is ready to vanish away" (Heb. 8:13). Chapter 9 of the book of Hebrews explains that the author had in mind the "ordinances of divine service and the earthly sanctuary" (verse 1, NKJV) that God established for the expiation of the sins of the people of Israel.

Hebrews 9 and 10 then go on to tell in detail that these specific services were no longer necessary because they were "a shadow of the good things to come" (Heb. 10:1, NKJV). That the Holy Spirit indicated "that the way into the Holiest of All was not yet made manifest while the first tabernacle was still standing" (Heb. 9:8, NKJV). Everything—all the ordinances and blood sacrifices—was symbolic. These things were, in a sense, a rehearsal for the real thing.

The book of Hebrews points out that if a person focuses on the physical manifestations of bringing gifts and offerings to the high priest as a type of bribe to gain favors from God, or is concerned only with what he or she eats or drinks, or in performing the various washings (oblations), then the individual has lost sight of the true worship of God. Such religious activities lost their meaning with the coming of the Messiah—"the High Priest of the good things to come, with the greater and more perfect tabernacle not made with hands, that is, not of this creation. . . . For if the blood of bulls and goats and the ashes of a heifer, sprinkling the unclean, sanctifies for the purifying of the flesh, how much more shall the blood of Christ, who through the eternal Spirit offered Himself without spot to God, purge your conscience from dead works to serve the living God?

"And for this reason He is the Mediator of the new covenant, by means of death, for the redemption of the transgressions under the first covenant, that those who are called may receive the promise of the eternal inheritance" (verses 11-15, NKJV).

As we have seen before, in ancient times people ratified covenants (agreements, promises) with animal sacrifice. They believed it took blood to make it binding. Exodus 24:5-8 confirms this. Verse 8 says: "Moses took the blood and dashed it on the people and said, 'This is the blood of the covenant that the Lord now makes with you concerning all these commands.'" But according to Exodus 32:1-19, the people violated the covenant a short time after its ratification.

God was calling for a people who would keep their promises to Him—a people whom He could depend on to pass the spirit of holiness down to the thousandth generation. In Exodus 31 God called craftsmen—Bezaleel of the tribe of Judah and Aholiab of the tribe of Dan—to construct the Ark of the Testimony. Scripture tells us that He "filled him [Bezaleel] with the Spirit of God, in wisdom, in understanding, in knowledge, and in all manner of workmanship" (verse 3, NKJV). Likewise, He put wisdom in the hearts of all the gifted artisans so that they could follow through with His design of the ark. And while He was giving orders to the workmen, He told Moses: "Speak also to the children of Israel, saying: 'Surely My Sabbaths you shall keep, for it is a sign between Me and you throughout your generations, that you may know that I am the Lord who sanctifies you. You shall keep the Sabbath, therefore, for it is holy to you. . . . Therefore the children of Israel shall keep the Sabbath, to observe the Sabbath, throughout their generations as a perpetual covenant. *It is a sign between Me and the children of Israel forever;* for in six days the Lord made the heavens and the earth, and the seventh day He rested and was refreshed'" (verses 13-17, NKJV).

Many claim that since we are now living under the new covenant, we no longer need to observe the seventh-day Sabbath that God established as an everlasting sign of the covenant between Him and His people. Instead, they argue that they can observe the first day of the week (Sunday) in honor of the Messiah's resurrection as their special day of worship.

But the Bible provides no support for such a view. Although we are living under the new covenant, it is our duty and privilege to honor and obey God's Ten Commandment law, including the fourth commandment that calls for the observance of the seventh-day Sabbath (Saturday) from sunset Friday evening until sunset Saturday evening (see Ex. 20:8-11; Lev. 23:32). Scripture declares that the Sabbath will be honored in the earth made new also (Isa. 66:23).

We find many references to the covenants God made with His people, and yet time and again the people broke these holy agreements—these oaths or contracts. And our heavenly Father, often in vain, would plead for His children to remember their promises, but they would not.

If this is true, who then are the covenant people?

When God called Abraham out of Ur of Chaldees (Gen. 12:1-3), He promised to make him a great nation in order that through him and his seed the Lord might bless all the nations of the world. It was God's divine purpose in calling the patriarch in the first place. He made a solemn covenant with him, and He confirmed that covenant to Isaac and Jacob. The Lord planned to give to all people the religion of heaven. He recorded His message and plan of salvation in the Bible, which the Jewish people would then share with everyone.

"Thus said the Lord:
Observe what is right and do what is just;
For soon My salvation shall come,
And my deliverance be revealed.
Happy is the man who does this,
The man who holds fast to it:
Who keeps the sabbath and does not profane it,
And stays his hand from doing any evil.
Let not the foreigner say,
Who has attached himself to the Lord,
'The Lord will keep me apart from His people';
And let not the eunuch say,
'I am a withered tree.'
For thus said the Lord:
'As for the eunuchs who keep My sabbaths,
Who have chosen what I desire
And hold fast to My covenant—
I will give them, in My House
And within My walls,
A monument and a name
Better than sons or daughters.
I will give them an everlasting name
Which shall not perish.
As for the foreigners
Who attach themselves to the Lord,
To minister to Him,
And to love the name of the Lord,
To be His servants—
All who keep the sabbath and do not profane it,
And who hold fast to My covenant—
I will bring them to My sacred mount

And let them rejoice in My house of prayer.
Their burnt offerings and sacrifices
Shall be welcome on My altar;
For My House shall be called
A house of prayer for all peoples.'
Thus declares the Lord God,
Who gathers the dispersed of Israel:
'I will gather still more to those already gathered'"
(Isa.56:1-8).

God intended that Abraham's descendants should be the channel through which He might reach the world in a special way. Israel was to bear witness to the Creator.

In Deuteronomy 4:5-8 Moses said: "See, I have imparted to you laws and rules, as the Lord my God has commanded me, for you to abide by in the land that you are about to enter and occupy. Observe them faithfully, for that will be proof of your wisdom and discernment to other peoples, who on hearing of all these laws will say, 'Surely, that great nation is a wise and discerning people.' For what great nation is there that has a god so close at hand as is the Lord our God whenever we call upon Him? Or what great nation has laws and rules as perfect as all this Teaching that I set before you this day?"

But since the people of Israel rejected God's words and His commandments, statutes, and ordinances, He gave this message to them through the prophet Jeremiah: "Go, make this proclamation toward the north, and say: Turn back, O Rebel Israel—declares the Lord. I will not look on you in anger, for I am compassionate—declares the Lord; I do not bear a grudge for all time. Only recognize your sin; for you have transgressed against the Lord, and have scattered your favors among strangers under every leafy tree, and you have not heeded Me—declares the Lord. Turn back, rebellious children—declares the Lord. Though I have rejected you, I will take you, one from a town and two from a clan, and bring you to Zion. And I will give you shepherds after My own heart, who will pasture you with knowledge and skill" (Jer. 3:12-15).

I particularly like what comes next in verses 19 and 20. God says: "I had resolved to adopt you as My child, and I gave you a desirable land—the fairest heritage of all the nations; and I thought you would surely call Me 'Father,' and never cease to be loyal to Me. Instead, you have broken faith with Me, as a woman breaks faith with a paramour, O House of Israel—declares the Lord."

Through Hosea God told Israel: "Then I will say to those who were not My people, 'You are My people!' And they shall say, 'You are My God'" (Hosea 2:23, NKJV).

Since Israel failed not only to live up to God's expectations but decided instead to keep the message and covenant to themselves rather than to carry His message to all nations and peoples, God told them that He would raise up others to do that. And the others would become His people.

Hosea was not the only one to issue a warning. The prophet Isaiah tells that God "shall come as redeemer to Zion, to those in Jacob who turn back from sin—declares the Lord. And this shall be My covenant with them, said the Lord: My spirit which is upon you, and the words which I have placed in your mouth, shall not be absent from your mouth, nor from the mouth of your children, nor from the mouth of your children's children—said the Lord—from now on, for all time" (Isa. 59:20, 21).

In Isaiah 65:1 God said: "I responded to those who did not ask, I was at hand to those who did not seek Me; I said, 'Here I am, here I am,' *to a nation that did not invoke My name.*"

So I read in these passages that those who keep the covenant with the Lord—whether they be the children of Israel by birth or through adoption, or through the Spirit of God whom they have received through repenting of their sins—are the people of the covenant and the sons and daughters of God. Many will be of Abraham's seed, but countless others will also join in the blessings of the book of life.

Thus, the answer becomes clear to the question "Who are the people of the covenant, the chosen people?" They are those who *choose* to obey God by keeping His commandments and having the Spirit of God within them. Some Christians call themselves the new Israelites, claiming that since the Jews chose to break the conditions of the covenant, He turned away from them and made a new covenant with the Gentiles. That is only partially true. Throughout the Scriptures, God offers the people of Israel a way back through repentance and heeding His commandments.

The New Testament asserts in Galatians 3:29 that "If you are Christ's [the Messiah's], then you are Abraham's seed, and heirs according to the promise" (NKJV).

This is the promise—the covenant—made to Abraham. Are then the Gentiles also Jews?

The New Testament teaches that Gentiles must become spiritual Jews. Does this also mean they must become circumcised in the flesh, as was required of Abraham's seed and household as a sign of the covenant? Some early believers in Christ said, "It is necessary to circumcise them, and to command them to keep the law of Moses" (Acts 15:5, NKJV). Peter, who himself was a Jew, answered that God had chosen him to take the word of the gospel to the Gentiles. Then he said: "So God, who knows the heart, acknowledged them, by giving them the Holy Spirit just as He did to us, and made no distinction between us and them, purifying their hearts by faith" (verses 8, 9, NKJV).

Many sincere, Spirit-filled people today believe they are the new Israelites or claim to be God's people. I have over the years visited and studied with many of them, including the Baha'is, the Jehovah's Witnesses, and the Mormons, among others. Yet when I was searching for a people whom I thought embodied the spirit of the Lord and I became acquainted with the Seventh-day Adventists, I knew I had indeed found a people of the covenant. As a result, I've joined the Seventh-day Adventist Church because they:

Believe in the Lord (YHWH).

Believe in the Messiah, Y'shua' ha-Mashiach.

Believe in both Testaments as one Bible, the Word of God.

Believe in the Ten Commandments, the unchanging law of God.

Believe in the Sabbath as a sign of the covenant between God and humanity, and observe it from sunset Friday evening to sunset Saturday evening.

Believe in the health laws given to Moses and do not eat unclean foods.

They named themselves "Adventist" because they believe in the return or second advent of the Messiah as King of kings. Through daily worship and study, they maintain their devotion and connection with God. And faithful to His Word, they are taking the message to the world so that "all the nations shall be blessed" (see Matt. 24:14; 28:19, 20; Rev. 14:6, 7).

What better Jew could God want?

When the Messiah returns at the Second Advent, He will take to heaven the faithful of all ages (1 Thess. 4:16, 17). All true believers who have their names in God's book of life will be saved (Rev. 21:27).

God's heavenly ledger records all the good deeds of "those that love the Lord." "The Lord has heard and noted it, and a scroll of remembrance has been written at His behest concerning those who revere the Lord and esteem His name. And on that day that I am preparing, said the Lord of Hosts, they shall be My treasured possession; I will be tender toward them as a man is tender toward a son who ministers to him. And you shall come to see the difference between the righteous and the wicked, between him who has served the Lord and him who has not served Him" (Mal. 3:16, 17).

When the Philistines seized King David in Gath, he asked God to have mercy on him, saying: "You keep count of my wanderings, put my tears into Your flask, into Your record" (Ps. 56:9).

Or shall your name be written into the book of sins? The prophet Jeremiah said: "Though you wash with natron and use much lye, your guilt is ingrained before Me—declares the Lord God" (Jer. 2:22).

But we have nothing to fear. For the blood of Jesus, the sacrificial Lamb for the sins of the world, will blot out all those references beside our names. He intercedes in our behalf. Daniel says that everlasting life awaits the faithful for having honored their Maker, and that all those whose names are retained in the book of life will share in the glorious reward of the righteous. "At that time, the great prince, Michael, who stands beside the sons of your people, will appear. It will be a time of trouble, the like of which has never been since the nation came into being. At that time, your people will be rescued, all who are found inscribed in the book. Many of those that sleep in the dust of the earth will awake, some to eternal life, others to reproaches, to everlasting abhorrence. And the knowledgeable will be radiant like the bright expanse of sky, and those who lead the many to righteousness will be like the stars forever and ever" (Dan. 12:1-3).

Those who have professed to be the children of God but who have persistently broken His sacred law will not share in life everlasting. Many will protest in the last days: "'Lord, Lord, have we not prophesied in Your name, cast out demons in Your name, and done many wonders in Your name?' And then I will declare to them, 'I never knew you; depart from Me, you who practice lawlessness!'" (Matt. 7:22, 23, NKJV).

Do you truly know the Lord God? Do you know His Son, Y'shua of Nazareth, the Messiah?

To truly know the Lord is to love Him. It is a lifelong, daily walk that not only can bring you true happiness and joy in this stressful world, but the hope and promise of life everlasting in the hereafter. I am both an ethnic and spiritual Jew through genealogy and by choice. In this book I have tried to give you references from the Holy Scriptures as well as through the testimony of my continuing life search for truth. If you are searching for answers to life's mysteries as well as for a guide to a happy, healthful, wholesome life, they can be found in God's own Guidebook, the Holy Scriptures, which includes both the Old and the New Testaments. I hope what I have presented here has provided you with a foundation. May your efforts to seek truth be richly rewarded.

As the Lord says through His prophet Jeremiah: "You will search for Me and find Me, if only you seek Me wholeheartedly" (Jer. 29:13). May your search for the Messiah also have a glorious conclusion.